THE SCOURGE

Keen Butterworth

THE SCOURGE

And it shall come to pass . . . for their worm shall not die, neither shall their fire be quenched. And we shall wrest from their waste a New Earth.

For Collin
Hope you will
enjoy this story,
Love,
Big Daddy

Terra Nova Books
SANTA FE, NEW MEXICO

Published by Terra Nova Books, Santa Fe, New Mexico.
www.TerraNovaBooks.com

ISBN 978-1-938288-52-4

For Nancy

Chapter One

GWEN SITS ACROSS THE TABLE BEHIND HER SCOTCH ON THE ROCKS, staring at me with those gray-green eyes—challenging as much as inviting an answer.

"I'm sure he didn't kill her," I say. "I've known Carlton for nearly two years. Even drunk he's gentle as Jesus. I'm going to Helena tomorrow to make sure he gets a first-rate lawyer."

"He didn't deny he'd killed her when Ralston arrested him yesterday."

"Carlton wouldn't have admitted or denied anything."

"Well, he'd better speak up for himself pronto," Gwen says, knocking down her drink. "Barney told me the slug they dug out of her was a .25-35 Winchester. Carlton's the only one around here with a gun like that. . . . Rumor was he'd been screwing her for a couple of months."

"I'm sure that was her idea."

"Yeah, with that streamlined body, I guess she got most anyone she wanted."

An image of Lila's partially devoured corpse flashes across my brain. I found her last Thursday over near Golden Meadows where I was fishing the South Fork. It was a warm day for late November. There were ravens . . . magpies. I walked up the draw where they were squawking. She'd been buried, but shallow, and something had dug her out. A bear from the looks of things. Part of the left side of her face was gnawed away—her eyeball gone—and a good portion of her arm and shoulder. Beneath the tatters of her shirt, her left breast had been ripped away from her chest and hung down on her rib cage. There was the stench. Maggots were seething in her suppurate flesh. . . . I try to wipe the image from my head.

"You guys want another drink? I've got to close the bar in ten minutes."

It's Jody. She owns the place, one of the three bars in Clark City.

"Well, do you want a midnight special or not?"

I tell Jody we've had enough, knock down my scotch and toss an Andy J onto the table.

Outside the air takes a deep bite. The temperature has fallen to around zero, and a few lazy snowflakes drift through the nimbus of the street lamp.

I ask Gwen if she wants to come over, but she says that Friday is a big day at the clinic, what with the flu epidemic and the slick roads: "If you're back from Helena, I'll come over tomorrow night."

Gwen is a nurse-practitioner and the town's only medico. She runs the county clinic on Shields Street, just the other side of the Forest Service Ranger Station. She has an ambulance and a list of volunteer drivers to call on when she needs to get patients to the hospitals in Helena or Great Falls. Since I'm close by and available, I've driven a number of times. That's how I got to know her—though it's no great shakes getting to know people in Clark City. The population is only seven hundred. Everybody knows everybody else and nearly everybody hobnobs at barbecues and the annual rodeo. Then, too, the bars in Clark City are like neighborhood pubs, real friendly, particularly Jody's and the Antler. The Stockman is more like a club—for ranch owners and foremen and the big wheat farmers.

It's a close-knit town, but nobody's felt the need to incorporate Clark City. The only streetlights are the three on Discovery Street that the electric co-op provides for free, and tonight it's dark—not even enough snow for a pale luminescence. So we make our way by memory and the stars over to Gwen's duplex on Colter Street. Spook, Gwen's black lab, hears us and starts whining and thumping his tail against the jambs. When Gwen opens the door, he leaps around us, then runs off into the dark to do his business. I kiss and hold Gwen while we wait for Spook to come back.

"Are you handling it all right, Jake? I know it must have been rough finding her like that."

I tell her I'm okay.

"I was in a war, remember? I just get flashes of her lying there half buried with her face and upper body torn all to hell and fouled with dirt. It wasn't pretty. And she was such a good-looking woman."

"Yeah, damned good-looking. I don't want to think Carlton could have killed her either. Tell him hello for me tomorrow. Tell him I'm sure things will turn out all right. They haven't found the gun. Anybody could have stolen it. . . . Do you have any idea who might have wanted Lila dead?"

"No. But maybe I can find out."

"Don't get mixed up in this mess, Jake. You can't tell what's going on. Randal is one tough hombre—have you seen him?"

Randal Turrentine is Lila's husband. He was in Bizerte when the sheriff finally located him. I'd heard that he had flown back to his ranch—he has his own Learjet and a landing strip on the prairie beyond the house—but as far as I knew, he hadn't been into town.

"I'm going out there Saturday after I've talked to Carlton."

"Stay out of it, Jacob. You can't tell. . . ."

"I'll be fine. Don't worry about me."

Spook has finished his business and is cavorting around our feet. I kiss Gwen good night and walk the two blocks over to my place on Pryor Street. There's a chill inside so I turn on the gas stove, a little cast-iron Jøtul I bought last year in Great Falls. Even though the bungalow has only four rooms and a bath, the old furnace doesn't keep it warm enough when the outside temperature gets down to zero or below. The Jøtul, with the ceiling fan I installed over it, heats the place in a jiffy. I warm my backside at the stove, then go in the kitchen and mix warmed milk with two ounces of Myers's Rum to help me sleep. For the last two nights Lila has been getting mixed up with Laura in my dreams.

Laura—my wife of twenty years. We were married during my last year of grad school. Then we'd made the rounds as teachers—Wesleyan, Oberlin, Williams—until I landed a position at Chicago. She had a masters in philosophy and picked up courses wherever we went. We'd tried to have kids, but no luck. The ob-gyn said it had something to do with Laura's tubes—something neither of us understood. We kept trying. Would have anyway: it was a good marriage, with the usual squabbles that kept us alive to one another but no major wars. Then, the year before last, she was gone. On our way home from a party, an eighteen-wheeler hit us out on the Skyway. Laura was driving. I was asleep. The police said the truck driver was going too fast, hit a patch of ice and flattened our car against the barrier. When I came to, every part of my body was crying with pain—I thought I could actually hear my legs and shoulder wailing. And there was Laura with her head nearly ripped off. I never even hoped she was still alive her face was such a mess. The reek of gasoline and crushed metal, blood and torn flesh. When they finally got the car door cut off and worked me out, the EMS boys said I had a broken leg and a dislocated shoulder, superficial lacerations to my face and body: I was going to live.

The next summer I resigned my position at the university. One of my older colleagues, a Montanan, had brought me out here twice on fishing trips twelve and ten years ago—once to the Big Blackfoot and once to Sun River. That year we stayed at the Bunkhouse. There's a photograph in the lobby taken during Teddy Roosevelt's first term in office, the same year Owen Wister's elegy, *The Virginian,* was becoming a national sensation. In the photograph cowboys slouch astride their steeds staring down the wide, muddy street at the camera, the monotonous opposing façades of wooden storefronts converging in the background. The town has settled into bucolic tranquility since then, but some flavor of the old frontier still hangs on. That's why I moved here two years ago.

The rum is not much help. My befuddled brain starts reeling fast, then slows, then speeds up again. Lila, Laura . . . Gwen. The worst is seeing Gwen like the other two, like three disfigured Graces, their faces mangled, their breasts ripped off. Then I'm spinning out of control, the room whirling around me . . . *you lie with your nose shoved into the grit, wheezing, trying to catch your breath, the stench of jungle rot pressing in on you like a malicious succubus. The platoon is pinned down in a sandy wash by machine-gun fire. You can tell by the ricochets that Charlie's aim is high. You have just given the order to keep heads down and crawl back to a secure position around the bend when the bastards start lobbing mortar rounds into the wash. It's one of your own M19s they've captured. Shit is flying everywhere. Terrifying HE fumes bite at your nostrils. Shrapnel is shrieking past your head. Guys are screaming for medics. Some are just screaming. A shell hits five meters away. You are down in a shallow hole that seems to turn to jelly. When you raise your head, there's Regis, his belly ripped open, staring with the fascination of a child at his guts coiling down between his legs. Hog slaughter, you think. Chitlins and tripe* . . . I'm hanging over the head puking and sobbing. I puke until there's nothing left in my belly. No rum, no milk, no food. Not even lining, it feels like. Just bile and a terrible emptiness.

Chapter Two

CLARK CITY IS SET OUT EAST OF THE FOOTHILLS JUST FAR ENOUGH FOR you to see the craggy snow-capped peaks of the Front Range beyond. The only tokens of civilization west of town are several big spreads, a scattering of dude ranches and outfitters, and the irrigation reservoirs. Beyond those lies the Great Grizzly Wilderness—two million roadless acres, comprising four or five mountain ranges, depending on how you count them, and the headwaters of seven major rivers. It is the largest natural wilderness in the lower forty-eight and one of our last havens for wildlife: grizzly and black bear, pronghorn and bighorn, mule and whitetail deer, moose and elk, wolverine, cougar, bobcat, lynx, pine marten and fisher. Beaver. Even a few wolves have stolen back down from Canada. Eagles and hawks rise on the thermals. Ravens. Owls. Trumpeter swans. Sandhill cranes. Multitudinous Passeriformes. The streams roil with trout and whitefish. Despite the persistent intrusion of hikers and pack trains of hunters and anglers, the region is not essentially different from when it served as hunting- and battle-ground for Blackfoot and Salish Indians.

The sparsely inhabited Missouri River plains roll away to the east of town, with big cattle ranches and wheat farms marking the way to Helena, a hundred miles to the southeast. Besides being the state capital, Helena is our county seat and the only other town in Ordway County.

This morning the hills hunker down under their brown-and-gray patchwork quilt, preparing for a long winter's sleep. Even the occasional junipers have a dingy, exhausted look. I'm half way to Helena when snow starts swirling down so hard I have to slow to thirty miles an hour. Fortunately my '86 4Runner is a lynx on snow. I stop to lock the hubs, then creep the rest of the way into the city, straining my eyes for taillights and oncoming headlights. By the time I pull up in front of the county sheriff's complex, the snow is six or seven inches deep.

Ralston Nichols is the sheriff. A tough bastard upfront but a decent guy underneath. He listens patiently while I tell him that Carlton couldn't have killed Lila.

"Maybe he didn't, Jake. But the evidence is pretty incriminating. The coroner thinks Lila had been buried for three or four days. Carlton's only alibi is that he'd been working on a barn out at the Circle 9. Puts him right there with plenty of opportunity to kill her and haul her out to Golden Meadows. We still haven't found the gun, but the slug being a 117-grain round nose .25-35 Winchester and the fact that he'd been frigging the woman since last summer—I asked him about that. He claimed that they had stopped having relations in October. He also said he thought his gun was still in his closet at the Bunkhouse.

"Christ, we turned his room upside down, looked everywhere. Searched his pickup too. All we found was that .270 he bought from Johnson Clyde last year. And a .38 midnight special. We're still looking. We'll find it if he didn't throw it in Gibson Reservoir—I expect that's what I'd a-done if I had shot her. If we don't find the gun soon, we'll have to let him go. . . . I don't think he shot her either, Jake. He's as mild-a-mannered card-carrying Blackfoot as I've ever met. Even drunk he's sweet as coffeecake. But the D.A. says we're going to keep him unless somebody posts bail. That ain't been set. Judge Harkness is holding the hearing Monday morning."

"What I wonder, Ralston, is whether you'd have arrested him on such flimsy circumstantial evidence if he weren't an Indian. I hear the D.A. is antsy to run for the Senate."

"Yeah, I hear the same thing. He seems to think we have enough evidence to make a case. . . . I do what he tells me."

"He must see this as a big opportunity. Turrentine is big-time money. Lots of political clout too."

"I ain't privy to his motivations."

I tell Ralston that I want to talk with Carlton. By the time I fill out all the paperwork and get in to see him, it's past two o'clock. He's standing at the back of the jail cell, looking out the window. I guess he thinks it's just the jailer because he doesn't turn around until Campbell says, "A man here to see you, Heavy-Eagle."

When he turns around, his eyes flick to high beam but he doesn't smile. Carlton is a good-looking Indian—six feet two or so and trim, without the blubbery layer a lot of Indians have. Last year I hired him to help me cut and hew Douglas fir logs for the cabin I'm building over near the wilderness. This summer, when the logs are dried out, he's going to help me raise them and put on a roof.

"How you doing, Jake?"

"I'm fine. The question is 'how are you doing?' Carlton."

"I'm doing okay. If it weren't for this stench of creosol. . . . I didn't kill her, Jake."

"I never believed you did. It's the rifle, and the fact you'd been sleeping with her. You never told me about that."

"I wasn't too proud of it. It was over anyway. I was out there in June reframing that old barn she wanted to save. She'd have me into the house every morning for coffee. One day when Buck was gone to town and Jeremy and Olivia were straightening up the guest-house, she took me up to her bedroom to ask about some changes she wanted to make in the bathroom—she wasn't wearing nothing under her robe."

Carlton tells me that Lila kept finding ways to get the two of them alone. She'd been real nice to him, but he got to feeling pretty bad about the situation with Mr. Turrentine paying him good money for the carpentry.

I tell him not to feel bad, that Turrentine could afford it.

"Did you know last week that she was missing?"

"I knew she wasn't at the ranch," he says. "The Land Rover was gone. But she was away for several days a lot of the time. I didn't think nothing of it. Buck was gone too. When he came back, he didn't say anything."

"She ever say anything that would make you think someone wanted her out of the way?"

"Naw, Jake. We didn't talk too much. Never had much time. She just told me her old man hadn't touched her in five or six years."

When I ask him about the rifle, he tells me the same thing he told Ralston. He hadn't used it at all since he bought the .270 from Johnson Clyde. He thought the gun was still in the closet. Besides, if he was going to shoot Lila, why hadn't he used his .38? It's pretty hard concealing a three-and-a-half-foot rifle: It would get in the way when you're lugging a body around.

Carlton is no dumb Indian. Nobody else had raised that question, though, now, it seemed an obvious one to ask. I make a note in the little farmer's notebook I keep in my jacket pocket.

After assuring Carlton that I'd hire a good lawyer to get him out of jail as soon as possible, I go downtown to Dick Latham's law office. Latham had done some work for me when I moved to Montana. He completed the forms for Laura's life insurance and negotiated the settlement with the van line's bonding company. Later he made sure the titles on my bungalow and the hundred acres I bought out in Finnegan's Gulch were in order. He tells me he doesn't do criminal cases but takes me to meet a friend of his, Jon Erickson, who has an office in the same building. Dick says Erickson is the best trial lawyer in Montana.

When I tell Erickson what I know, he says, "People constantly surprise me, Mr. Battle. Particularly in these clandestine affairs. You can't predict what people will do, even your best friends—people you think you know inside out."

"Carlton wouldn't have done it. He swears he didn't have anything to do with the killing. I can tell he's shaken, despite the stolid mask. He really liked the woman. She wasn't just some lay."

"From his point of view, that's what I mean."

Erickson asks me a lot of questions about how I know Carlton, how he got involved with Mrs. Turrentine, and so forth. I tell him all I know, but he knows more about Randal Turrentine than I do. He tells me Randal's got big interests in Enron, an enormous energy company down in Houston. Also has his irons in a dozen other fires, probably more than the IRS knows about. Erickson had gotten wind the FBI was investigating Turrentine. Maybe concerning drug trafficking and money laundering.

"I tell you this in confidence, Mr. Battle—if you are a lawyer, you hear these kinds of things when someone like Turrentine moves into the area. There's a network—you get connections as far away as Houston . . . and New York."

Snow is still falling at six o'clock when I leave Erickson's office. Down here in Last Chance Gulch it's about twelve inches deep. I stop at the Wrangler Bar and call Gwen. She's not at the clinic or her apartment, so I leave a message on her answering machine telling her I'm holing up at the Lewis and Clark Hotel because of the snow and won't be back in Clark City until sometime tomorrow.

The kitchen at the hotel is the best in town. I place an order for veal Marsala to be served in an hour, then head into the bar for a little conversation with Wilson the bartender and a tumbler of Glenmorangie Claret Wood from the special bottle he keeps for me in the cabinet.

"Why didn't you bring Miss Jefferson?" Wilson wants to know. "She's one of my favorite ladies. I always look forward to seeing the pair of you—especially her."

"She had to work today. It's the busy season at the clinic—flu, wrecks."

"Well, make sure you bring her next time or you're not getting served."

"It's coming," I say, when he asks about my latest novel. "But I haven't had much time to work on it lately. This Lila Turrentine thing sort of diverted my attention."

"Yeah, damned waste. I saw her several times. One hell of a woman."

Wilson tells me that Lila had come into the bar a month ago with a guy he'd never seen before. They'd sat in the far corner arguing about something.

"Big ugly guy. I never seen him again. . . . Mr. Turrentine, he used to come in here on occasion. Ain't seen him in a year or more. Too bad. He tips like a blackjack player. What you reckon someone would want to kill her for?"

I tell him I don't know, but if he ever sees the guy she'd been with to give me a call. I hand him a card with my phone number and email address before heading back into the restaurant.

After the veal Marsala and a B&B, I feel like I'm ready for sleep, but half the night I lie awake running scenarios through my head. Who would want to kill that beautiful woman? Her husband? Evidently she'd been screwing around on him for years. Probably his fault. He was damned near thirty years older. She was thirty-six, Ralston told me. Why had Turrentine kept her here in Clark City when their home was in Houston? As far as I knew, she'd left Montana only a couple of times in the last two years. At a party after the rodeo the summer I moved to Clark City, I'd danced with her, tried to charm her, I guess. We talked for a good half hour, but I didn't know much more about her at the end of our conversation than before we'd started. Later I heard a lot of scuttlebutt: She'd been a high-fashion model before she married Turrentine. Even acted in a couple of movies. She'd had plenty of visibility in *le beau monde*. A man like Turrentine was bound to have lots of enemies. Maybe one of them was trying to get at him by killing his wife. Maybe she wouldn't give Turrentine a divorce and he wanted out—without having to pay an arm and leg. Maybe he'd found out something about her past he couldn't deal with. Maybe he was having cash flow problems and had taken out a big insurance policy on her. Maybe she had something on her husband and had been blackmailing him. There were lots of possibilities. Maybe one of her former lovers. I didn't know but one besides Carlton. That was Scott McIntire, who owned the sawmill and lumberyard up in Guthrie—not a likely candidate. Maybe the wife of one of Lila's lovers. But carrying her all the way out to Golden Meadows and stealing Carlton's gun to shoot her with—a woman wouldn't go to all that trouble. Maybe I'd been seeing too many movies, reading too many detective novels. Nothing was making sense. Lila's death didn't make sense. Burying her fifteen miles from the nearest road made no sense. Shooting her with Carlton's rifle and then hiding it made no sense. The whole business made no sense. Life itself made no sense. That was the state of mind I'd reached when I finally nodded off to sleep.

Chapter Three

GWEN AND I ARE LYING ON THE MATTRESS WE'VE PULLED INTO THE living room in front of the Jøtul stove.

"That was good, Jacob. I'm glad you made it back from Helena. Must have been a bear in all this snow."

"Yeah. I got behind a snowplow. There's a foot and a half out on the level—must be five feet alongside the highway. . . . Roll over, I'll rub your back."

She loves having her back rubbed after we've made love. I like rubbing it. She has the most sensual skin—a peachy white that seems thicker than most people's, creamy smooth, softer and more elastic. A perfect complement to her dark auburn hair. She has a little Indian blood in her too, enough to give her high cheekbones and a high, handsome forehead. She also exudes the most erotic aroma. I lower my nose to the top of her head and take a deep breath. I rub for a while, then turn her over.

After the next round she's down between my legs, fondling my parts, rubbing her cheek along my inner thigh like a cat.

"What the hell is this?" she asks, raising her head to look at the big scar just under my gluteus maximus and running her fingers over it. "I've never noticed it before."

"A memento of the *Indochine* jungles."

"Jesus, how did it happen?"

"A fragment of a Bouncing Betty one of my privates stumbled over."

"A Bouncing Betty?"

"A Chicom landmine. They jump up in the air about four feet before they detonate."

"Jesus, a couple of inches to the left, you'd have been a eunuch."

"A couple of meters closer, I'd have been a corpse."

"You're not over it yet, are you, Jacob? You're still wrestling with it."

"I don't think you ever get over it. Things just get in between. I don't like talking about it."

"Okay," she says. "Tell me more about Carlton. What did you find out?"

I tell her about my interviews with Ralston and the lawyer. When I mention what Wilson told me about Lila coming into the bar with a stranger, she lights up.

"About a month ago, yeah, I think I saw him. A really ugly guy with pockmarks all over his face. And big, maybe six-four, six-five. She was in the Jag sedan in the post office lot. I walked over to say hello. Then this guy came out of the post office and got into the passenger seat. Nodded to me but didn't say anything. Lila seemed a little embarrassed. Said she was in a hurry and drove off toward the ranch. I don't think he was one of her *intimates*."

When I mention what Carlton told me about Turrentine not touching Lila for five or six years, Gwen lights up again and says Lila had told her the same thing. They'd been pretty close a few years back, after Lila had fallen off her horse and wrenched her knee. After Gwen treated her at the clinic, they'd gone out to lunch together and shopping in Great Falls several times.

"I found out she was seeing some colonel stationed at the airbase. She was frank about it . . . told me that her husband knew about her affairs and didn't much care. She hinted that she'd had trouble down in Houston—with affairs, and probably alcohol. Maybe drugs. I think Turrentine bought the ranch to get Lila away from Houston, and from New York—they had a place on Central Park West."

She moves her head over onto my shoulder: "Sometimes when

I wake up in the morning, I thank old Natos I'm not rich. That I have to work hard for a living. That keeps me out of trouble—except for you, of course".

"How am I trouble? I'm not rich: I just have a lot of money."

This morning Gwen fixes a breakfast of salt herring, eggs, and grits. I have to order the herring and grits special from Virginia—they've never heard of such fare out here in the land of over-easies and hash browns on sirloin. After initial revulsion, Gwen has come to like the Old Dominion cuisine. We eat a leisurely breakfast, reading snippets from the newspaper to each other—mainly about Monica Lewinsky and prophecies of doom concerning Y2K breakdowns at the end of the year. I clean up the kitchen while Gwen takes a shower. Then I get the bathroom. After a shower and shave, I call out to the Circle 9 to see if Turrentine will talk with me. Buck Wallace answers the phone. He's Turrentine's right-hand man here in Ordway County. I guess he'd been assigned to keep Lila out of trouble by not letting her stray too far, or stay too long, away from the ranch. He tells me to hold on while he checks with his boss. After a few minutes he comes back on the phone.

"Mr. Battle, he says for you to come on out. Can you take a late lunch with him?"

"Sure. Tell him I'll be there between one-thirty and two."

Olivia serves us chiles relleno with a wonderful green sauce. She's a Mexican-American the Turrentines brought up from Houston to be cook and housekeeper.

"I hope you like Southwestern fare, Mr. Battle. Olivia makes the best rellenos I've ever eaten. Beats even the best chefs in Santa Fe and Taos. Her mother was raised in the San Luis Valley in Colorado."

Olivia looks at me and blushes, bends forward at the waist, then hurries back out to the kitchen.

"Call me Jake, Mr. Turrentine."

"Sure, if you will call me Randal. You're the former professor, aren't you? A professor turned novelist. You were at the barbecue out here summer before last, if I remember correctly. Did you know my wife well? Sheriff Nichols tells me you were the one who found her over in the wilderness. I'm sorry you had to bear that."

"I thought it was a bear that dug her up from the looks of things. But Charlie Left-Hand, who went out there with Ralston to examine the area, said it was a wolverine. There aren't many of those around anymore. Vicious little creatures, I've heard."

"I saw her in the morgue in Helena. Even after they'd cleaned her up, she wasn't a pleasant sight. To think that such beauty is so fragile. Despite its toughness and resilience, the human body is vulnerable to traumatic injury at every moment. We tend to forget that. It's a sobering realization."

Turrentine speaks about his wife's death in a detached manner. He looks me in the eye as he lays his fork on the rim of his plate: "Was there something you wanted to tell me that the sheriff doesn't know?"

"I don't know anything he doesn't," I say. "But Carlton Heavy-Eagle is a friend of mine. I don't believe he could have killed her. I think somebody is trying to frame him. He hasn't used that .25-35 Winchester since he bought his new rifle last year. He thought it was still in his closet at the Bunkhouse."

"The sheriff said he'd been sleeping with my wife, Mr. . . . Jake. From my experience such entanglements can cause any amount of irrational behavior. My wife was a beautiful and intoxicating woman—she could stir up a lot of primitive emotions and behavior. I know—I was completely enthralled when I married her. When I found out about her first affair—two years later—I could have killed her. I considered having an 'accident' staged, but sanity prevailed. There would have been inquiries. Bad for business. Divorce was out of the question. . . . Would you like another cerveza? The Negra Modelo is very good with rellenos, don't you think?"

I tell him, no, that I've had enough, wondering why "divorce was out of the question." Was Turrentine Catholic?

"Were you married before, Randal? Or is that any of my business?"

"It's no secret. Yes, I was married before. Once. For fifteen years. My first wife, Ethel, died of cancer twenty-three years ago. I've been taught the hard way what a fine woman she was."

"What about Mrs. Turrentine . . . Lila?"

"That's no secret either. She'd been married twice. Twice divorced. But I told her when we married—the Church, you know. She knew divorce was not an option. Under the circumstances I could have had the bishop annul the marriage, but that would have been unpleasant. I'm very much in the public eye down in Houston. But that's enough about our lives, Mr. . . . Jake. I'm sure Sheriff Nichols will solve the case. He seems to be a competent investigator. I've told him all I know. I don't think he needs any help, though I've offered a sizable reward if anyone can lead us to the killer. . . . Would you care for a flan? Olivia makes an excellent flan."

I decline, thank him for the meal, and excuse myself, thinking *lead us to the killer*? Evidently Randal didn't believe Carlton killed her either.

"I hope I wasn't prying," I say on the way out. "Finding her like that was a shock. I can't help but be curious."

"Not at all, Jake. If you hear anything relevant to the case, I hope you will relay the information to Sheriff Nichols."

I assure him I will and take my coat, which Jeremy is holding out beside the front door. Jeremy is a mulatto, distinguished despite his portly figure. He gives me a pointed look when he's turned away from Turrentine, as if he has more to tell me than to take care on the drive back.

"The roads might be slick now they been scraped," he says. His accent is distinctly southern Louisiana.

I think how Southern blacks and whites of a certain caste seem always to recognize and are drawn to one another. Maybe Jeremy does have something to tell me.

Randal walks out to the car with me.

"You can tell the people in town—they're probably wondering—that I'm having Lila's body cremated. We'll take her back to Houston. I'm planning a memorial service for her down there. She liked living up here, but I think her spirit was more attuned to urban Texas."

On the way back to town, I mull over the conversation with Turrentine. He obviously wasn't grief-stricken about Lila's death, but that didn't make him guilty. He hadn't hesitated to tell me about his and Lila's past. If he'd really wanted a divorce or annulment, he could have arranged one without much public embarrassment—unless she had some trump card that he was afraid she'd play. He could easily have arranged for her death, but my instincts told me he wasn't involved in the murder. Beneath that suave exterior, he seemed baffled by Lila's death. Or was he good enough to make me believe that? A man in his position would have to project all sorts of nuances in his business and political relations. I needed to learn more about Randal Turrentine. There was something in the man's demeanor that bothered me. I just couldn't put my finger on what.

"When they moved here, Jake—that was in ninety-two—it seemed the town had been injected with new energy. We had been certified by the larger world, transformed from a high-plains village into a place to be reckoned with."

Gwen and I are lying on the mattress in front of the Jøtul stove again. On the muted television across the room, the Bears and Packers are slogging it out, playing in Green Bay in five inches of snow.

"Mrs. Thompson was seventy-five years old and couldn't run the ranch any longer, and neither of her kids could oversee the operation. Sam is a doctor in L.A. and the other one, Larry, is a lawyer in Tucson. Everybody thought what a pity it was. The Circle 9 is the biggest spread in the county and had been in the Thompson family since the mid-1880s. Nobody wanted it passing into the hands of strangers, but nobody around here could afford it. We didn't have any idea who Turrentine was, but when word got out he'd bought the ranch, half the town became instant experts on his biography . . . and Lila's. There were stories about big money buying spreads over on the Ruby and in Paradise Valley. How these strangers came in and marked off their boundaries with orange posts and No Trespassing signs. Wouldn't let their neighbors hunt or fish on the land. Wouldn't have anything to do with the community. Brought in their own people to run the ranch. Henry Thompson Junior, the country singer, had just done that over in the Big Hole. When people heard the Turrentines were building their own airstrip out on the Circle 9, everyone figured they'd do the same thing. Instead Randal and Lila came to the rodeo that summer, dressed Montana style—as conceived by Neiman Marcus. They tried to, and did, fit in. Randal can be awfully charming when he puts his mind to it. And Lila, well, all she had to do was stand around and smile. They were both instant hits.

"The next week Louise Duncan spread the word that the Turrentines had set up an endowment for the Clark City Library—to the tune of one hundred thousand bucks—and ordered eight PCs to be installed the following month. That fall Lila became a silent partner in Lydia Stokes's gift shop and helped her pick out stylish clothes and gifts. Helped her decorate and stock the shop as well. Randal was away most of the time, but Lila was in town nearly every day checking her box at the post office and shopping. She bought a lot of groceries and canned goods at Tomaski's store—stuff she probably didn't need. Same at Larry's Hardware.

"Lila was always bright and friendly. One day she came into the Antler while I was having a sandwich and ordered a drink. There was a poker game going on, which Lila watched with obvious interest from the bar. When one of the players had to leave, Phil Turner invited her to join the game. Lila held her own. Even won a few pots. After that she'd go into the Antler once in a while, and if there was a game, she played. It turned out she knew a lot about horses too. She was raised on a farm near Lewisburg, West Virginia, and had ridden horses nearly all her life. She'd been on the equestrian team at Sweet Briar College.

"She told me a lot of this stuff after we became friends. Before she graduated from college she was offered a job as a model in New York; one of the fashion magazines had done a piece on college girls at the Virginia finishing schools, and she'd been *discovered.* It was three or four years before she hit it big—a cover for *Vogue*—but after that her career took off.

"Lila married Tom Hanover, the movie actor, about that time. The marriage didn't last a year. Then she married a Hollywood producer, whose name I don't recall. The producer got Lila a couple of good roles in so-so films. *Venus in Wraps* was one of them—you might remember that from back in the mid-eighties. . . . Anyway, their marriage lasted a little longer, two or three years, I think. Then she met Randal Turrentine. He was still young enough to be dashingly handsome, and rich as the Shah.

"Lila told me that she'd grown tired of the modeling/acting rat race. Randal was a ticket into another world. It was a good ride for a while, but after a year-long honeymoon, Randal had to get back to business. He was gone for long periods of time: to Europe, the Orient, South America, Africa, Australia. He seemed to have global connections and investments. Lila was left alone with lots of money to compensate for her loneliness. Later, she found companions. She started getting sloshed a lot and hinted to me that maybe there was a problem with drugs.

"I guess she became an embarrassment and liability to Randal in Houston. So he bought the Circle 9 and made it as comfortable a place of exile as one can imagine. I guess she did straighten out for a while, and he stayed around a good bit that first year to make sure she did. She certainly seemed fine to us—beautiful and gracious. Everybody was flattered by her attention. If there had to be new owners on the Thompson ranch, we couldn't have chosen a better pair of landlords and neighbors."

When Gwen takes a break to go to the bathroom, I slip in the kitchen for a couple of beers and a bag of chips. On the way I check the score of the ballgame. Green Bay has an eleven point lead: Favre has just completed a thirty-five yard touchdown pass to Antonio Freeman.

After we get settled again, Gwen continues her tale of Clark City social life after the arrival of the Turrentines: "On July the Fourth of the next summer they had a big barbecue at the ranch and invited the whole county. Anybody who could come was welcome. God knows how many beeves they cooked. Most of the other food was catered out of Great Falls and served under a big tent canopy they had erected in case of rain. Besides the food there were kegs and kegs of beer and a full bar. I couldn't have paid for the spread with a year's salary. They also hired a bluegrass band out of Boulder—Tim O'Something and Quick Rise. You ever hear 'Stars and Stripes Forever' and 'America the Beautiful' played bluegrass style? It was a wonderful time! Never before had there been such a shindig in Ordway County.

"The July Fourth barbecues became an annual event. News traveled up and down the Front Range, and the crowds grew larger every year. The horseshoe-throwing competition even made news in the *New York Times* one summer. There were celebrities from all over mingling with the crowds. Timothy South was there one year, and Elizabeth Sawyer. If you saw somebody you didn't know, you just automatically assumed they were celebrities whether you recognized their faces or not. . . . You went to the one year before last—I remember dancing with you—before we became a couple."

Neither of us knows why there wasn't a barbecue last summer. Gwen heard it had something to do with a big financial mess down in Houston.

"I don't know when she started the affairs again," she says. "The first I heard of was with Scott McIntire up in Guthrie. Then there was the colonel, and I guess others, and then Carlton. Too bad for him he has such a pert, narrow little ass."

Chapter Four

"I DON'T THINK I COULD HAVE TAKEN THAT CREOSOL MUCH LONGER," Carlton says as we leave the jail headed back to Clark City. "Thanks for getting me out, Jake."

"Don't mention it. I'm going to need your help raising those logs this summer. Besides, it was Jon Erickson who got you out."

As Erickson had pointed out at the hearing, there wasn't much evidence against Carlton. Even though Winchester stopped making them sixty-five years ago, there are still a few .25-35s around. If they didn't find the rifle, there would be nothing to tie Carlton directly to the killing. They'd have to prove the gun was a match to have a case.

"You've never locked your door since I've known you," I tell him. "Anybody could have taken that .25-35 from the Bunkhouse."

"Yeah, but I guess Judge Harkness woulda liked to have held me until I begun to rot. He don't much like Indians."

After our initial exchange Carlton just sits looking out the window. He's not much into long conversations. I met him shortly after I moved to Clark City. While I was looking for a house and then negotiating for the bungalow on Pryor Street, I stayed at the Bunkhouse, where he's a permanent resident. Carlton is a loner. He works on various construction jobs in the area and hires himself out on small jobs as an independent laborer. He is a first-rate carpenter—meticulous, if a bit slow. Most nights I'd see him at the bar in the Antler, which is directly across the street from the Bunkhouse. He always drank alone and looked kind of lonesome. We had in common the fact that we lived down the hall from one another, so I introduced myself. Over the next month we drank together two or three nights a week. He seldom got drunk but paced himself, one drink after another, until Phil chased him out at closing time. I was working on a novel about the Crow Indians—the one I haven't finished yet—and I asked a lot of questions about Indian life. Of course, being a Blackfoot, Carlton didn't care for the Crows—they were ancient enemies—but he told me what he knew, and something about his own tribe, reluctantly.

"You sure do ask a lot of questions, Jake," he would say when he got fed up with talking, and I knew the session was being brought to a close.

Nonetheless, over the next several months his own history dribbled out in our conversations. He had been born on the Blackfoot Reservation a hundred miles north of here. He was "one hundred-percent Piegan," he told me. His parents were honest folks—both of them worked for the tribal government—and they made sure he got a high school education. Afterward he took courses in plumbing, wiring, and carpentry at the technical college. He was good enough at electronics that the career counselor got him a job at Boeing's factory in Everett, Washington. He spent a year feeling homesick, then married a girl from Snohomish—pure Irish. They had a couple of kids, but then things began to fall apart. He started drinking heavily and lost his job with Boeing. The wife decided he wasn't a fit husband, or father, and filed for divorce and custody with child support. Carlton came home, but there was nothing for him on the reservation, so he ended up in Clark City on a big construction job for the state. He'd gotten used to the town, even though he didn't particularly like it. He controlled his drinking—usually. And he sent his support checks to Seattle every month. The wife was remarried to a lineman for Puget Sound Power & Light, so Carlton didn't worry much about the kids. Although the judge had given him visiting rights, he hadn't seen them for two years. He had contracted the endemic Native American diseases—spiritual lassitude and alcoholism. I had thought that I could help raise him out of his funk, so I became his friend and hired him to help me with the cabin. And then this damned Lila business came along.

When we get to the Bunkhouse (the sign out front and the advertising call it the Bunkhouse Inn, but nobody around here has called it anything but the Bunkhouse since it was built in 1909) Bob Taylor is sitting in the lobby watching television, some talk show on the disasters that could come with Y2K. The guests are two self-appointed experts on the subject. Bob gets to watch a lot of television; he tends the place while his wife Bunny works as a surgical nurse in Helena. Bob and Bunny bought the Bunkhouse seven or eight years ago and have fixed it up nicely—new siding, balconies, storm windows, fresh paint in the rooms, new furniture as they can afford it. Bob is working on the plumbing and wiring, when the spirit moves him.

"So you're out, Carlton. Welcome back. I guess your buddy there's got all manner of pull in Helena. . . . Wait a second. I want to hear what this jerk has got to say about the blackouts and computer snafus we're gonna have."

So we all listen until the commercial break.

"Ralston and Barney turned your room upside down," Bob says. "Bunny wanted to clean up the mess, but I told her you'd want to put things back where you were used to keeping them. Maybe you didn't want anybody else going through your stuff either."

"Thanks, Bob. That was thoughtful of you."

"You betcha. Anytime, Carlton."

Bob goes back to his show and we go up to Carlton's room, which *is* a mess. All the drawers are pulled out and emptied. The contents of the closet are strewn all over the floor. The mattress is leaning against one wall. But what Carlton is most upset about is a photograph—a long-lens shot of a handsome wolf peering out from behind an Engelmann spruce. The frame and glass are broken and the picture pretty well torn up.

"What the hell they bust up my picture for? I liked that picture. I think I'll sue Barney. I bet he was the one did it."

"It wasn't your picture, Carlton. It was Bunny's. Gus Fox gave her all the pictures in the Bunkhouse for display. . . ."

"Yeah, but she said I could keep it. You know Gus told me he took that picture down on the Dearborn. You ever hear of wolves on the Dearborn? There are some up around Polebridge, but I never heard of any down here. . . . There was a cousin of my grandfather who lived down there back in the '30s. They say when he died, he turned into a wolf. Then this woman from New York moved into his old cabin. They say she turned into a wolf too and joined him. I bet that wolf is one of their descendants."

"You don't believe that crap?"

Carlton gives me a facetious look: "*And the third day he arose again from the dead. . . .*"

"You don't believe that malarkey either, do you? I'll get Gus to print you another copy. I'm sure he still has the negative."

"Leave it, Jake. I'm already in debt to you up to my haunches. Don't offer to do nothing else for me for a while. That lawyer must have cost a few C-notes. I'll be the rest of my life trying to get you paid off."

"I told you, I got more money than I'll ever need. Ever want. You're welcome to a hunk of it right now."

"How much money you got, Jake?"

"I already told you last summer."

"I just want to hear it again. It consoles me to know I've got a rich friend."

"Two weeks ago you had a rich girlfriend."

"Christ's sake, Jake, that was all over. She wasn't my girlfriend anyway. Just a lay. I never fooled myself. She tried to make out we were more than that, but I knew I didn't mean anything to her. It was good though. Best I ever had. But come on, tell me how much money you've got in the bank."

"One million, nine hundred and ten thousand dollars."

"Jesus!"

I tell him one million, two hundred thousand of that came from the accident—life insurance and the settlement: "It's America's new way of making millionaires: wisely purchased insurance policies and litigation."

"Seems to bother you a lot, Jake."

"Maybe it does. So let's drop it."

"Sorry, I wasn't trying to needle you."

Carlton quietly picks up his clothes for a while then says he wants to go out to Golden Meadows tomorrow and see where I found Lila. Maybe there was something Ralston and Charlie didn't see.

"I'd like to find the bastard who shot her, Jake. I'd make sure he didn't rub out anybody else ever again."

"Okay, Carleton. I'll go. It doesn't look like I'm going to get any work done until this Lila business is settled anyway."

We rent a couple of horses at the K&L Ranch and ride along the north side of Gibson Reservoir into the wilderness. Past Sun Butte the countryside opens up along the South Fork of the Sun River. Most of the snow from last week has melted off the prairies, though it's still a half-foot deep in the woods. It's beautiful country. The grass is all tawny brown with patches of snow here and there. Outlining the prairies are dense stands of lodgepole, Engelmann spruce, and Douglas fir, with some ponderosa scattered among them. Along the river the big cottonwoods stand sentinel, waiting for winter to pass so they can spring forth into leaf again. High up on the surrounding hills, barren aspen trees huddle, their trunks white as chalk. In summer the stretches of prairie along the river are shimmering green and spangled with flowers—lupine, paintbrush, penstemon, arnica, and bistort. In early fall, with the cottonwood and aspen turned bright gold, the country is so beautiful it makes your throat dry up. It's my favorite place in the world to fish—cutthroat and rainbow up to twenty-four inches, and lots of brook trout further back up the West Fork.

We turn south and ride down to Golden Meadows. At first I can't tell in which draw I'd found the ravens squawking, but then I recognize a couple of features and lead the way back into the woods. As far as I can tell, nobody's been in here since last Friday. We find the spot easily—there are piles of fresh earth sticking up through the snow. When Carlton dismounts and pokes around the grave site with a stick, I start getting flashes of Lila's mutilated body.

"Wonder what he dug the grave with, Jake. Wasn't a shovel. Maybe a big knife, or an ax. No wonder he didn't bury her very deep."

He looks around until he finds a wolverine track, which he points out to me, but there's nothing else of interest, so we go back out on the prairie. Carlton rides in circles around the mouth of the draw, moving farther and farther out onto the flats, all the while looking intently down at the ground. After several circuits he dismounts and picks up something. When I ride over, he holds up a shell casing—a .25-35.

"It's mine," he says. "The son-of-a-bitch shot her out here, then dragged her up in the draw."

"How do you know it's yours?"

"These old casings I use four or five times. I can tell by the marks on them—they're like old friends. It's hard to find ammo anymore so I get Louie Schmitz to reload them for me. He does it cheap."

When I ask him where he got the antique Winchester in the first place, he says his grandfather's uncle stole it from a ranch near Shelby back around the turn of the century.

"It used to shoot good," he says. "The lever action is real sweet. But the rifling is getting worn. Sometimes the bullet don't spin right."

I say that whoever shot her probably did it at close range. He wouldn't have had to worry about the bullet keyholing. According to Ralston, the bullet had entered through her left breast.

"If I ever catch the son of a bitch. . . ."

"Come on, Carlton. You've found what you wanted. These short days, it'll be dark when we get back to the K&L. What are you going to do with the casing?"

"Leave it here where I found it. They didn't find it the first time, they ain't likely to find it again. I'll put it under a rock to make sure they don't."

"It might have the prints of the man who shot her."

"I doubt it, but I know it's got mine. I ain't taking that chance . . . unless you know how to get the prints checked without going through Ralston and the D.A."

"You know I don't."

Carlton wants to look around a little more and shows me two sets of horse prints near where the shell kicked out.

"So? They could be Ralston's and Charlie's," I say.

"No. I saw theirs over near the draw. These are different. I think these here are Lila's little Arabian. These others are a bigger horse."

While I'm writing in my notebook everything Carlton has said, he makes a few more circuits on foot. When I ride over to where he's standing, he holds up his hand with two more shell casings in the palm. They're still bright and shiny.

"Look at this, Jake. They're .32s. What do you reckon?"

"I don't know. What do you reckon, Carlton?"

"A hunter wouldn't have a .32. Could have been a backpacker brought one along for protection."

"Target practice?"

"Two shells don't make target practice."

He slips the casings into his shirt pocket and says it's time to go.

It's dark when we get back to the K&L and around seven when we drive into Clark City. I call Gwen. She's not home, so I call the clinic. She's working late, but says she'll be finished in an hour.

"Want to meet Carlton and me at Jody's for a steak? I'm treating."

"Sure. I'll come on down when I'm finished."

Carlton and I are into our third beer when Gwen arrives. I tell her about visiting the grave and finding the horse prints but leave out the shell casings.

"Carlton says one set of prints is probably Lila's Arabian. I'm going to call Ralston tomorrow. Maybe he'll get Turrentine to let us come out to the Circle 9 and check. Somebody out there has got to know something. More than they told Ralston the first time. Buck Wallace, or Jeremy."

"Well, I doubt Randal will let them tell any more than he wants you to know," Gwen says.

"Jeremy will if I can get him by himself."

After we eat, Carlton excuses himself, saying he needs rest: he's got a new job to start on tomorrow. Gwen and I walk to her duplex to get Spook, then over to my place. After we settle in bed, Gwen gives me a concerned look.

"You seem pensive, Jake, like something else is bothering you. You okay?"

"It's just this business of Lila's murder. It's been nagging away at me. Seeing that grave again today. . . . Lila's dead, and it sure looks like somebody killed her on purpose—premeditated. But there are other kinds of murder. I guess in some ways, all of us are murderers. People die because of our carelessness, or irresponsibility, or selfishness."

"Like all the starving kids in Africa? Civilians in Bosnia and Iraq? That's just the world. It's life, Jake. Send some money to UNICEF or one of the relief charities. It's sad, but we all have to live with that kind of guilt. It's so abstract and disconnected."

"Sometimes it's a lot more personal and direct."

"Is the accident bothering you again?"

"Probably. But it's not always easy to tell what it is. Sometimes it's just a relentless nagging despair, not a particular thing. Maybe it's about something that happened in Vietnam."

"Something you haven't told me?"

"Yes . . . no, I haven't."

"You can tell me now if you think it might help."

I doubt it will help, but I tell her anyway. I call it "The Story of the Bamboo Hootch":

My last month in 'Nam, my platoon was sent up to a little village along the Rao Quang River where they'd been having trouble with snipers and someone lobbing mortar rounds over onto Highway 9. Intelligence said Charlie was also storing M18 Bouncing Betties somewhere in the area. They'd been digging up a lot of them recently, and they'd gotten pretty good at it because we no longer found as many dead Cong blown away while they were trying to disarm the mines. Recently they'd been setting a lot more of our Claymores than they were Chicom Bouncing Betties and Toe Poppers. My platoon drew the assignment to reconnoiter and clear the area. They chopped us in from Ta Bat in two Hueys, and we looked around for half a day without finding anything—no gooks, no encampment, no tunnels, no M16s, not even a booby trap. I radioed in several times on the PRC-25. Keep looking, the captain said. Our intelligence claims to be very recent. So we looked some more. Just out from the village there was a rice paddy with a bamboo hootch on the other side that looked suspicious. I sent four men around the east perimeter of the paddy, where there was cover. Three of us went straight across at staggered intervals. We left six men in cover on the backside of the paddy for support. We're about half way across when a DP 7.62 opens up, spewing rounds all across the paddy, little pocks of water popping up all over the surface. The three of us in the open drop down behind a shallow dike. We can't see where the fire is coming from, so I yell to the guys on the flank. Rennie yells back that it's coming from the hootch. I yell for him to make sure. Hell, I'm sure, he yells back. I just seen the bamboo wedged open where he's sticking the barrel through. So I give the order to blow the place apart but to avoid hitting the water buffalo standing ten or fifteen meters to the east of the hootch. I hear Cabniss's 'pig,' the M60, open up with the baseline—chotachotachotachot. Then a lot of accompaniment from M16s—k-chat, k-chat, k-chat, k-chat, k-chat, k-chat. When I figure the place is pretty well torn up, I give the signal to cease fire. I wait five minutes then send Stovall forward. There is no fire. He walks up within a few yards of the hootch, fires a couple of burst, then flings the door open. What do you see, Stovall? A woman and two kids chewed up pretty bad. We look all over the hootch—it smells like shot-up rabbits. Then we look in the jungle on the other side. We never find Charlie or a DP or M16s or anything. Whoever had been shooting from wherever had even taken his shell casings with him. When I fill out the report that night and hand it to the captain, he reads it over, then looks up at me. Hell of a war, ain't it, Left-enant? He tears the report in half and files it in the shit can. Then he says he'll make sure an accurate report gets to headquarters company: You might even get a medal, Jake. Now you go on down to the mess and get a drink. However many it takes to get you to sleep tonight. . . .

"That woman and her kids were all torn up," I tell Gwen. "They didn't look human, more like rag dolls that had been chewed on by a dog. I'll bet a week hasn't gone by since without an image of them smeared on the floor of that hootch flashing through my brain."

"It's a matter of intent, Jake. You had a job to do. How could you have known there was a woman with her kids inside the hut? You thought a sniper was in there. It wasn't like My Lai."

"They were dead. Real dead. . . . Just being an arrogant American, thinking you could improve the world by killing a bunch of Vietnamese commies. . . . I'm not sure intent—conscious intent anyway—has much to do with guilt. Most of the people I killed intentionally over there don't bother me. They would have killed me. . . . If there were a Saint Peter, I wonder what he'd have to say on the matter. . . . I wonder how many unintentional murders it takes to equal an intentional one, or vice versa. . . . Maybe whoever shot Lila hadn't intended to when he took her out to Golden Meadows. If he had, he'd probably have carried a shovel."

"I don't know, Jake. It's a very complicated problem, and I'm tired. Let's get some sleep. I've got a long day at the clinic again tomorrow."

Chapter Five

About fifty miles south of Clark City, State Route 200 crosses the Continental Divide at Rogers Pass. A Forest Service sign beside the road informs you that the pass is 5,610 feet above sea level. Additionally, it states that on January 20,1954, a miner's thermometer nearby registered the lowest temperature ever recorded in the lower forty-eight states—minus 70 degrees Fahrenheit. It probably got colder but there was no way to prove it: The thermometer broke. This morning I'm driving Route 200 to Missoula to see Dave Lieberman, an old friend who teaches economics at the university. We were colleagues at Williams in the '80s. When I called yesterday to ask if he'd help me do some research on Randal Turrentine, his first words were that Turrentine was one of the hundred wealthiest men in the country: he couldn't possibly be clean.

"Sure, we can dig up a lot of dirt on the rascal," Lieberman said. "It was his wife you found, wasn't it. What's going on? Are you investigating the case?"

At Rogers Pass, I stop to stretch and take a piss—too much coffee with breakfast. Also I want to see how cold it is. Probably minus 25 or so: If I arc my spit high enough, it freezes before it hits the ground, but my piss remains a steamy yellow stream burning into the snow. I stomp around for a few minutes getting the kinks out of my muscles and try to imagine what minus 70 would feel like. The locals say you can't tell the difference after it drops below minus 30; you just have to be more careful not to get frostbite.

"Always keep moving," is the general advice. "If you've got the right clothes on, you'll stay warm enough."

I'm not dressed for arctic weather. My nose and cheeks are nipped and my kidneys are feeling a chill, so I jump back in the 4Runner, switch off the overdrive and drift down the mountain. I'm now in the drainage of the Big Blackfoot River, where Norman brought me fishing some years back. It was pretty disappointing. The stream was heavily silted from all the clear-cutting in the valley, and there just weren't many fish. We had to move over to the Clearwater, where he had a cabin, and even there the fishing was only so-so. Fortunately, there's been a concerted effort to restore habitat here in the valley, and the river is noticeably clearer now. Most of the clear-cut sores are healing over. The Blackfoot alliance even blocked an attempt to locate a gold mine at the head of the valley. Tim Free, who floated the river last spring, told me that the fishing is getting good again. I think I'll come over and do some shadow casting in memory of Norman this summer.

Between Lincoln and Ovando, I pass the sign for Brown's Lake off to the left. I call it Hugo's Lake because that's where the poet Richard Hugo used to fish. He and I had dinner together back in the early '80s. I'd thought from the publicity that he was a fly fisherman, but no, he told me, a pole fisherman.

"I float around Brown's Lake in a skiff, drinking beer and loading my hook with worms. Poems come to me that way, and once in a while, I catch a fish."

The guy must have poured down five or six drinks while we were having dinner, and inhaled one cigarette after another. Finally killed him. He just fell over in the classroom one day. But he'd already made sure the "work" would be carried on. His students tell me he was one hell of a teacher.

The Big Blackfoot valley is a lot warmer than Rogers Pass. A lot warmer, too, than the plains at Clark City, where arctic air comes knifing down across the Canadian Shield. The Blackfoot is a tributary of Clark Fork, which is a tributary of the Columbia River. Over on this side of the mountains, you get West Coast weather: warmer and wetter. The clear sky gives way to a thin overcast. The forest changes: The deeper you get into the valley, the more big trees loom above the road, dense stands of Douglas fir, western larch, and ponderosa. I admire the scenery until I get to Bonner and Milltown, where the sawmill is ripping up logs. Lumber is stacked everywhere, most of it probably going to the Orient. I ramp up onto the interstate, anxious to get to Missoula.

Missoula is getting too big, but it's still a nice town. The university is about the right size—it doesn't dominate the city—and downtown is still viable. But the west end, where all the new growth is metastasizing, is pretty awful, overtaken by shopping malls and tract houses. It's become *anywhereville,* as we used to say back in the '60s. Fortunately I don't have to go through that part of town. I slip off the interstate a few miles from where I got on and drift down to the campus, where I find a parking space a couple of blocks from Dave's office.

He gives me a hug and hands me a folder.

"Here, just the usual Who's Who promo stuff. But I called a friend who teaches at Rice, and he's going to send what he can dig up by email, probably next week. Betty's fixing us lunch over at the house. She's anxious to see you."

Betty was Laura's best friend when she and I lived in Williamstown. She gives me a kiss and steps back for an appraisal when Dave and I walk into the kitchen.

"You look healthy, Jake," she says.

She asks after Gwen, whom she met in August when she and Dave and their daughter Gail visited me in Clark City.

"Why don't you two come over during the holidays this year?"

I tell her Gwen has family in Wolf Creek we've made plans to have Christmas with.

"Well, try to get over sometime during the break."

Betty gestures toward the table, so we sit down and she serves lunch. She wants to know about the murder.

"We read about it in the paper. About your finding her," she says. "I guess you've already told Dave, but I don't want to depend on him for the gory details."

So I tell them about finding Lila. About Carlton. About Turrentine. I've finished the spiel by the time Gail gets home from school, so I have to retell a cleaned-up version for her. After dinner, when she's gone off to do her homework, we finally get around to Laura.

"I miss her, Jake. I miss knowing she's alive somewhere . . . somewhere I can call her and we can talk, like we used to after you two left Williamstown. Dave gave me hell about the phone bills. Sometimes I wake up in the night now imagining that I'll call her. Then I remember that grisly wreck. God, what you must have gone through. . ."

"Have some consideration for Jake's feelings, honey."

"He can handle it. I know Jake. You're strong. You're over it, aren't you, Jake?"

"No, I'm not over it. But I'm getting on with life. I haven't tried to bury it. I try to let the pain take its course. Writing helps. Gwen helps a lot. But I'm not over it."

We reminisce about old times in Williamstown. The cross-country skiing parties on Greylock. Hiking in the Berkshires and Green Mountains. The summer we rented a cottage together for a month in Eastport, Maine. Concerts at Tanglewood. Trips into Boston for Red Sox games. By the time we decide to go to bed, my head is swirling with memories of Laura. I try to get them under control. It's still hard for me to understand that Laura is gone and won't return to my life. Sometimes she seems so alive in my head. Laughing and crying. Fresh and vibrant. Then sometimes she comes at me like a banshee, eyes red with rage, shrieking:

"You've been fucking someone, haven't you, Jake? You're not the same Jake. You're some other Jake, aren't you? You're not my Jake. That's why I'm dead."

I wonder if she ever told Betty about her suspicions, though she never said anything to me. It's just in my imagination that she accuses me, her face torn all to hell.

About four years ago I'd been assigned a new research assistant, a lovely, lithe, very bright girl from Evanston. Her name was Lillian—a dedicated student who wanted to write her master's thesis on Theodore Roethke. I gave her plenty of work to do in the library, which she always completed impeccably, in record time, then came back for more. As a reward, I'd take her out for beer a couple of times a week and talk about Roethke. She wanted to know everything I'd found in the collections at the University of Washington and Penn State. She had sandy blonde hair falling over her shoulders. She'd sit across the table with her head tilted, looking at me through or around the wisp that always hung over her right eye. I'd start a poem, she'd pick it up and finish it: "I wake to sleep . . . ," "the world is for the living . . . ," "I knew a woman. . . ." One night I walked her back to her car in a lot near my office. We'd had three or four beers each and kept bumping into each other. She giggled. Standing under some trees, I took her in my arms and kissed her, buried my nose in her hair. She smelled like a baby.

"God, I wondered when you were going to do that," she said.

We went to my office and got it over with on the rug behind my desk. From then on it was stealing time, stealing beauty. One Saturday when I told Laura I had to work in the library, I took a room in a hotel down near Grant Park, on the twenty-fifth floor where we could look out across the lake. I don't know if I was in love, but I was as moony as an eighteen-year-old kid.

Strange thing—at first the affair with Lillian energized my relationship with Laura. It was exhilarating. I'd get home after work and practically throw her down on the bed and make love until we were both exhausted.

"I don't know what's gotten into you," she said, "but I sure like it."

So did I. It was like I was master of a harem—a harem of two beautiful women. Several times I almost told Laura about Lillian, but I didn't. Then things began to change. I began to resent the time I spent with Lillian. It was taking me away from my work, and I began to realize it was interfering with my relationship with Laura. I could tell Laura had sensed that something was wrong. But I'd still sneak off with Lillian, though I began to feel like a cad and started drinking too much. One night after a party, Laura confronted me.

"Jake, you didn't used to drink so much. Is something bothering you?"

No, I told her . . . maybe pressure in the department. I hadn't produced much scholarship lately. But people were flocking to my lectures and I was spending more time writing fiction and poetry.

"Well, don't think you have to get drunk to project a macho image."

At the party the night of the wreck, I got pretty soused—enough that Laura wouldn't let me drive. So I sat in the passenger seat in a kind of stupor, staring into the oncoming headlights, and at the tail lights as cars zipped around us. Then I woke to the shrieking of bones—and there was Laura with her head nearly ripped off.

When she comes at me in my dreams, eyes on fire, I grab her and try to explain, but there's nothing to explain. All is done. All is finished. I stand helpless as she floats off into the night.

Chapter Six

THIS MORNING BEFORE BREAKFAST I READ THROUGH THE PHOTOCOPIES Dave gave me the day before yesterday. All of them have pretty much the same information, the usual bio digest. *Who's Who in American Business* is the most extensive:

> Randal Lamar Turrentine. Born 1933, New Orleans, LA. Father: Anthony Mark Turrentine, owner of dry-cleaning business. Mother: Louisa Evangeline Lamar Turrentine. Received B.S. in Economics, Tulane University, 1955. Married Ethel Lovett Rosetti, 1961. Made initial fortune wildcatting out of Shreveport in late 1950s and early '60s. Moved operations to Houston, 1967. Diversified interests: cotton and wheat brokerage; small arms manufacture and trade; savings-and-loan expansions; aerospace technology; nightclub owner. In '70s acquired large holdings in Arabian-American Oil Company. Developed philanthropic interests: Houston Museum of Fine Art; Houston Opera; Pasadena Children's Hospital; Greater Houston Urban Planning Coalition. In the '80s invested heavily in American software technology and Japanese automotive and electronics industries. Married actress Lila Godwin Byrd, 1988. Acquired large holdings in Enron Energy Corporation, 1992. Listed in *Forbes* magazine's 100 wealthiest men in the United States, 1997.

I hope Dave's friend at Rice can find something explaining how Randal made so much money so fast. Dave says he'll forward the information by email as soon as he receives it. Meanwhile I'm going to find out what else the sheriff has come up with. He wasn't too happy when I called Wednesday to tell him about the horse tracks Carlton found out in Golden Meadows.

"What are you two messing around out there for, Jake? Carlton had better keep his nose out of this. The D.A. is just looking for another reason to haul him back in."

According to Ralston, Charlie Left-Hand saw some horse tracks as well, but the sheriff didn't see any reason to associate them with the murder.

"Lots of people ride through there, particularly in hunting season. You were riding through there the day you found her."

"I was walking. . . ."

I asked Ralston to get the okay from Turrentine for Carlton and me to go out and look at Lila's horse.

"Okay, Jake. But you tell me what you find. And keep a halter on Carlton. He could still be in deep trouble."

I read the newspaper while I finish my coffee. More prophecies of doom about Y2K. More dirt on Monica Lewinsky and Bill Clinton. I look up at the clock: 7:15 a.m. Maybe Carlton is still at the Bunkhouse.

When I get there, he's in the shower. I wait in his room. When I tell him my idea about going out to the Circle 9 and looking at the horses, he says he's already been.

"Went yesterday," he says. "I'd left some tools out there in the barn. I called out and talked to Buck. He said Mr. Turrentine had gone to El Paso on business but left word for you to come on out if you thought you could learn anything about the murder."

Carlton knew I was in Missoula, so he'd looked around a little when he went to get the tools. It took him a while to find Lila's Arabian—she was down by the creek.

"Those were her tracks," he says. "Same nail patterns. Same nick in her right forehoof. I think the other horse was the big bay—looks like some kind of cavalry breed. They got ten or eleven other horses. I couldn't be sure. I asked Buck if she had ridden off with anyone Thanksgiving week, but he didn't know. At least he said he couldn't remember her riding anywhere but there in the ring. She did that most every day."

Carlton thinks that Buck knows something he's not telling.

"He won't look me in the eye. Maybe he thinks I killed her. He's never liked me. I don't like him either. He's a creep. Lila told me he was supposed to keep tabs on her. Probably kept a log of who she was fucking. She thought it was kinda funny."

Carlton and I go across the street to Annie's Cafe for breakfast before he heads to the job he has lined up for today, helping Tim Free replumb his kitchen and bathroom.

"He's got the most screwed-up connections between his supply and the water heater and the sink and the bathtub. Somebody must have been drunk when they plumbed it."

While we're sitting there, we see Buck Wallace drive by in the big Yukon with ⑨ painted on the door. He stops down the street at Orville's garage and fills up with gas, then drives off toward Helena. After breakfast I walk over to the garage and ask Orville if Buck said where he was going—I needed to see him about an emergency diesel generator Turrentine said he'd sell me.

"Said he had errands to run for Mr. Turrentine in Helena. I don't guess you'll catch him today, Jake."

I drive back over to the bungalow and clean up, then stop by the clinic to tell Gwen I'm back from Missoula.

"I would have called you last night, but I didn't get in till eleven-thirty. I'm going out to the Circle 9 this afternoon."

"What for, Jake?"

"Buck went to Helena this morning, and Randal's away on business. This is my chance to talk with Jeremy while there's no one else around."

"Watch out, Jacob. You could be wading in deep water. Make sure you know where you're stepping."

Gwen thinks that beneath all his urbane civility, Randal is a ruthless bastard and somehow involved in Lila's murder.

"Oh, I was thinking last night," she says. "You know Naomi Winslow, Ben Winslow's daughter? Well, since Ben was running the ranch for the Turrentines, Lila decided several years ago to hire his daughter to keep the horses. She grooms them and exercises them when they need it and keeps the tack. I think she goes out there every morning before school, and I know she checks on them in the late afternoons and makes sure they're fed. Their ranch is only about seven miles from the Circle 9. I know her pretty well. I could go out there with you to talk to her sometime. Maybe she knows something—particularly if Lila was riding with someone that week."

It's a good idea, I tell her. Then I ask if she wants to ride up to Guthrie tonight for dinner at the Log Cabin. "We could take in the movie after that. You know what's playing?"

"No, but I'd like to go. I need to get out of town for a few hours. This last week I've been called six times at night, twice after twelve. Flu's going around."

We agree I'll pick her up at her apartment at five-thirty, then I head out to the Circle 9. It's one o'clock, and the only vehicles around are the GMC pickup and the Super 350 Ford truck. On my way to the front door, I look in the garage windows. The Jaguar sedan is parked in the first bay.

Olivia answers the door.

"*Buenas tardes*, Señor Battle. Señor Turrentine, he is not here."

I tell her it's okay, that I want to talk with Jeremy. She gives me an uncertain look, then goes back in the house and calls him. I hear Jeremy's heavy tread coming down the hall.

"Oh, it's you, Mr. Battle. Come on in. I guess Olivia has forgotten her manners. You know Mr. Turrentine is away on business, but come on in. Come on back. I need to turn the disc player off."

Jeremy leads the way to a big room that's a library as well as a kind of music studio. The sound system is quality stuff—big Infinity tower speakers, a Denon powerhouse, an Onkyo disc player. Sidney Bechet's "Wild Man Blues" is playing at high volume.

While he fiddles with the controls and puts away the disc, I shuffle through the CD cases on the cabinet top: King Oliver, all the OKeh Louis Armstrongs, Fats Waller, lots of Basie, early Billie Holiday, Coleman Hawkins, Art Tatum.

"Mr. Turrentine lets me play these things whenever he doesn't require my services. . . . I'm from New Orleans, you know. Mr. Turrentine and I have known each other a long time. He loves this music too."

"Are you a musician, Jeremy?"

"Used to be. I was a pianist. Pretty good too, if I might brag a little. I even made a couple of LPs back in the sixties."

"You don't play anymore?"

"No, sir. I was sort of—how shall I say it?—cut out of my profession."

He holds his hands up, palm down. A nasty scar runs across the back of each hand.

"Jesus, how did that happen?"

"A man was upset with me. A Creole gentleman named César Lebeau—he was in the rackets. He had this thing for a little lady that sang in the club where I played piano. She was a pretty cream-colored gal with a voice that would send you into a trance. He was always after her, but she wouldn't have anything to do with him. Told him to get out of her life, she didn't want no trouble. Made him mad. Somehow he blamed it all on me—thought I was her sugar man. Couple of times he cornered me outside the club and threatened me. Said he'd cut my throat if I didn't stop messin' with his girl. I told him she wasn't anything to me but a friend and a wonderful singer I played accompaniment for. He wouldn't listen to reason. Had it stuck in his head I was the cause of his groin- and heartache. One night his henchmen grabbed me behind the club and forced me into a car. One of them stuck a pistol in my ribs. They took me somewhere out in the country around Bayou Cane.

César was waiting for me in an old, dilapidated Creole cottage I guess they used as a hideout. He told me he had warned me but I wouldn't pay attention. Said there wasn't but one way to make a nigger pay attention. Two of his strong-arms held me, while he used a straight razor on the backs of my hands."

There is obvious pain in Jeremy's voice, but he's not seeking my sympathy, just telling his story. He goes on to explain that Mr. Turrentine had loved his music and used to come in three or four times a week to listen back when he was in college. Later, in the '60s, Turrentine would drive down from Shreveport with his wife to hear Jeremy play. He even helped Jeremy get a contract with Fantasy Records.

"When he heard about how I'd been cut, he came down immediately and took me to the Ochsner Clinic in Jefferson, where the doctors tried to put my tendons back together. But my fingers never worked right after that."

Jeremy tells me that about two months after the cutting, Lebeau and his two henchmen were found floating in Pass Manchac. All three had been cut and dismembered where it really hurts—César's penis was stuffed down his throat. The murders were never solved.

"The papers said it was probably some kind of gangland payoff," Jeremy says. "Maybe I should have felt sorry for César and his boys, but I never did. Sometimes I wish I'd been asked to help with cutting off their parts. . . ."

Turrentine has taken care of Jeremy ever since, bringing him to Houston, where Jeremy worked in Turrentine's nightclub lining up jazz groups to play there.

"Sonny Rollins and Ornette Coleman and John Coltrane and Sam Rivers. I even got Miles Davis when he had that group with Herbie Hancock, Ron Carter, Wayne Shorter, and Tony Williams. But I didn't much like working there and not being able to play. There were a lot of people worked for Mr. Turrentine I didn't care much for either. When he bought this ranch and needed someone to take care of Mrs. Turrentine, I asked him to let me come up here and work. At least it's away from Houston—even if some of the trouble did follow us up here."

When he asks if I want to hear him play, I think he means he'll play the piano for me—there's a baby grand on the other side of the room. But he turns and walks over to the bookcases and takes down an old LP in its jacket. Across the front is "Jeremy Toussaint: Studies in Jazz Piano." He slips the red, translucent record out of the sleeve and puts it on the turntable.

The first piece is the old Gershwin standard, "I've Got a Crush on You." We listen to it, and then "I Can't Get Started" before Jeremy lifts the tonearm. The playing is lush, like Errol Garner but more sophisticated harmonically. There's some Art Tatum, and maybe a little Thelonius Monk, in Jeremy's style. I think I can hear the stride, much complicated, going all the way back to James P. Johnson.

"That's great stuff, Jeremy. I wish I could have heard you back then."

"Yes, sir. . . . It's like I'm listening to someone else play. It's hard for me to remember that I could play like that. . . . But that's enough of my past. You came to talk about something else."

"It seemed last time I was out here that you might have something to tell me."

"I do. But I don't know quite where to start."

"You could tell me first about the big guy with the pockmarked face. Several people saw him with Mrs. Turrentine."

I take out my little farmer's notebook and a pen and take notes while Jeremy is talking. He tells me that about a year ago, around October, the guy started showing up. First he came out in a rented car—from Great Falls, Jeremy thinks. The man was ugly, and tall. About six-six or seven.

"You ever see that big, ugly guy played in the James Bond movies? Called Jaws, I think. He looked sort of like him. Real scary. His face just wasn't put together right. He didn't stay but three or four hours. Mrs. Turrentine took him to the airstrip out there in the Land Rover. They rode up and down the runway a couple of times. When they got back, he went over to his car and got a little bag of something and handed it to her. Then he got in the car and drove away.

"About a month later, the same man came again, by airplane this time—one of those little things we used to call a Piper Cub, but it was probably some other kind. I don't know much about airplanes."

This time, Buck Wallace was with Lila when she met him out on the airstrip. The man hadn't stayed long, maybe thirty minutes. From the house Jeremy couldn't see what went on, but when Mrs. Turrentine came back, she was carrying a small suitcase. The next morning she and Buck had gone somewhere in the station wagon and hadn't returned until the following day.

"I can't say what was in the bag—it was like one of those overnight bags—but I did notice a change in Mrs. Turrentine's behavior for the next few days. She spent a lot of time in her rooms—she has a kind of suite upstairs. Olivia took food up to her, but she didn't eat much. I saw her only once or twice that week, but I knew it was cocaine. I saw lots of that down in Houston at the club. That's one of the things I didn't like about working there. I've toked my share of 'tea,' as we used to call it. But this snorting cocaine—that's evil stuff. I could see it in her eyes. You couldn't miss it—sort of glazed over."

When Lila finally came out of her suite, she started riding her horse every day, going to town, back to her regular activities. Jeremy never did hear the big man's name, but Lila call him "Bet" or "Bat" or something like that a few times. The man also had an accent Jeremy couldn't place. Maybe Central Europe—Hungarian or Romanian. His visits continued every month or so—but never when Mr. Turrentine was at the ranch. Same routine: He'd usually land and take right off again, but sometimes he'd stay around for three or four days. Whenever he brought a 'shipment,' Buck and Lila would go somewhere in the station wagon later—delivering the drugs, Jeremy supposed.

"When Miss Lila came back, she usually shut herself in her rooms for two or three days. Then she'd come out and go right back to her normal activities. Sometimes I thought I should tell Mr. Turrentine about what was going on, but there was Mr. Buck. . . . It just wasn't any of my business. Mr. Turrentine had known about Lila for a long time: she'd been picked up a couple of times by the police in Houston. Once coming back from Matamoros, she was caught with a whole mess of pills and Mr. Turrentine had to fatten a lot of pocketbooks to get her out of that one.

"The next time I saw that man was the week before Thanksgiving. He drove that time. Mr. Buck and Miss Lila shut themselves in the parlor with him for about an hour. There were a lot of raised voices like they were arguing, but I stayed back in the kitchen with Olivia and didn't hear what was said. When they came out, Mr. Buck and the man went off somewhere in the station wagon and Miss Lila went out and hooked up the horse trailer to the pickup. She'd stayed down at the barn for a while and then she left too.

"It was Saturday when they left. The man, Bat, he came back on Monday with the trailer and went down to the barn. Then he left in his car. That's the last I saw of him. Mr. Buck, he didn't come back until Wednesday. Mrs. Turrentine never did come back."

Jeremy is sure Turrentine didn't know anything about Bat or that Buck was involved. He'd overheard Buck tell Turrentine he thought Carlton had killed Lila because she was going to dump him.

"Or she wouldn't give him the money she'd promised. . . . Something like that," Jeremy says. "I wouldn't tell you any of this, Mr. Battle, if I thought Mr. Turrentine had anything to do with the murder."

"Have you said anything to Mr. Turrentine about the big guy?"

"No, sir. I've been afraid to. It's Mr. Buck. He's sort of . . . unpredictable. He told Olivia and me if we ratted on him, he'd do us worse than what happened to Mrs. Turrentine. He said that Bat would come back and make us real sorry. I know I should have said something to the sheriff, or at least told Mr. Turrentine, but I couldn't with Mr. Buck hanging around the whole time. And I was afraid if I told Mr. Turrentine what I knew, he'd have Modell kill Mr. Buck and get himself in trouble."

"Who is Modell?"

"You've seen him, haven't you? He's Mr. Turrentine's bodyguard. He never lets Mr. Turrentine get out of sight or hearing range. He's not a big guy. Kind of medium height and build. But he can handle himself. I saw him in action down in Houston a couple of times. He's fast with his fists. I hear he's even faster with a gun."

I have never seen Modell, who must have been out of sight when I had lunch with Turrentine last Sunday. Maybe he was around when I saw Randal other times, but I'd never noticed him. I write down Modell's name and put the notebook away in my jacket.

"I'll keep all this to myself as long as I can, Jeremy. But the sheriff is going to have to know soon. I'll try to keep you out of it, but I'll make sure the sheriff knows Buck Wallace had something to do with the killing."

I give Jeremy my phone number and tell him to call if he needs me or if he finds out anything else.

"How does Olivia feel about all this business?" I ask him.

"She's real scared, Mr. Battle. Her husband was killed in some drug-related business down in Houston. She knows how out of hand things can get."

"Can you drive, Jeremy?"

"Yes, sir."

"Can you get a set of keys to the pickup and keep them hidden?"

"Yes, sir."

"If things get too hot, you and Olivia get out of here. Call me, then drive to town."

On the drive to Guthrie, I tell Gwen what I learned from Jeremy.

"That big guy is scary, Jake. I never liked Buck Wallace. When I went out to the Circle 9 to have lunch with Lila, he was always around, like he was keeping tabs, making sure I wasn't a bad influence . . . or wasn't going to steal the silver."

"I'm going to call Ralston tomorrow. I guess I can get him on Sunday. I just want to make sure he doesn't put Jeremy and Olivia in danger. Randal is going to have to know about this too. Jeremy doesn't know when to expect him back—said Buck would know, but I've got to watch my step there."

The roast beef *au jus* is very good at the Log Cabin. It's their specialty on Saturday nights. And unlike most family restaurants in Montana, the salads are not just iceberg, cucumber, and wedges of hothouse tomato. They use Boston and endive and even mesclun when they can get it, with a nice raspberry vinaigrette. They don't have a liquor license, but you can bring your own. Gwen has brought a good, inexpensive red Bordeaux *Cru Bourgeois*. When we top off the meal with apple pie and a cup of coffee, neither of us feels like going to the movie, which, we learn, is some Disney thing anyway.

"Why don't they bring *Heartland* back?" Gwen says. "I'd go see that again. I wasn't here, but when they released it back in the early '80s, it ran nearly a whole year at the Roxy. People went to see it seven, eight times."

She tells me it was filmed just outside town—"Guthrie's claim to fame. That and Jack Horner's dinosaurs."

We're just getting ready to leave when Scott McIntire comes in with his wife and daughter. He sees us and nods but guides his family to a table in the adjoining room. I had thought last week that I should talk with him about Lila's murder, but now, after all Jeremy has told me, I figure Scott won't have any information of value. I also figure his wife would be real sensitive on the subject. If Ralston wants to talk with him, okay. But I'm not going to cause the guy any trouble. We pay the bill and leave.

On the way home we discuss the fact that there are no Hardee's or McDonald's or Burger Kings or any other fast-food chain in either Guthrie or Clark City.

"I hope they never get here," Gwen says. "They're a damned creeping dietary evil. Think of kids eating that crap, getting addicted to it. Fat, fat, fat, and more fat. It's almost as bad as smoking. And their promotions and advertising are just as insidious. Get the kids in and make them crave the Big Macs and Whoppers and breakfast biscuits. . . .

"They will, though. They'll get here. It's like a metastasizing tumor. Those big chains are going to eat us all up eventually. What the hell can we do? Particularly when our big hero, Willie Jeff Clinton, gets photographed patronizing them."

"Promote a civilized cuisine," I tell her, "and don't let our own kids get close to those places. Maybe evolution will step in. The kids that become habituated will get so obese they can't have sex. They'll die out like the dinosaurs. . . ."

We're talking food and Darwin, when, suddenly, about ten miles south of Guthrie, an ancient two-and-a-half-ton truck comes barreling over the top of a hill straddling the centerline. I had seen the headlights—still on high beam when the truck starts downhill—and pull as far right as I can on the narrow pavement. Even so, I can see it's going to hit us. I swerve onto the shoulder just as the truck rushes past. Four Indian kids are in the front seat and four or five in the bed, yelling drunkenly and waving to us as if it's just a game they're playing. By the time I stop the 4Runner, we're down in the ditch in a foot of snow.

"Goddamn it! Those kids are going to kill somebody, besides themselves."

"Not us, thank God! That was nice driving, Jake. Great reflexes for a man your age. Fifty-two, fifty-three? How old are you anyway?"

"I'll tell you my next birthday."

"We ought to report that truck."

"I will. It looked like a sixty-three GMC. Maybe Ralston or the state police can find out who it belongs to. There can't be many of those left around."

I get out to see if the car is damaged, but everything looks all right. The 4Runner has heavy-duty suspension and lots of clearance.

I lock the front hubs and get back in, still a little shaken. I put the transmission into 4-low and pull back up on the highway. About five miles down the road, I feel Gwen tense up.

"Jake, there's someone in trouble over this hill. Down near the gravel pit, I think."

Gwen has this uncanny sixth sense. It's the damnedest thing. Once we were driving through Simms on our way back from Great Falls when she tells me to turn off the road down this side lane. There's a big double-wide set back in a grove of cottonwoods.

"In there," she says. "Someone's in trouble."

There are lights on inside. Gwen goes up and knocks on the door, but no one answers. She tries to look in a window but can't see anything. She motions for me to come with her. I find an empty five-gallon paint bucket around the side of the trailer and move it under a window so I can get high enough to see inside. A woman with iron-gray hair is lying face down on the floor. I knock on the window. No response. I have to break one of the three slot windows in the front door and reach through to flip the latch. The woman is still alive but entirely unconscious. Gwen thinks she's had a stroke. We call the hospital in Great Falls and tell them to send an ambulance out to the trailer, give them the address and instructions to bring a magnesium sulfate IV. Then Gwen turns the woman on her left side, makes sure she is breathing regularly, and covers her with a blanket.

It turns out the woman did have a stroke and would probably have died if Gwen hadn't made sure the woman got the magnesium sulfate IV. Today the woman is living in the nursing home in Guthrie. Her speech is a little slurred, but her mind is still sharp, and she walks two miles every day. Gwen goes by to check on her once a month.

Now I approach the area of the gravel pits cautiously. I can't see anything abnormal, but then Gwen says, "Stop right here."

We both get out with the big power light I carry in the 4Runner and look over the embankment. Sure enough, down in the gulley a green Ford Explorer is resting on its top in a snowdrift.

"Anybody there?" I yell.

"Please help. I can't get the door open," a woman's voice answers.

She's not badly hurt but says her husband is unconscious. It takes me fifteen minutes to pry the door open with a tire iron. A dazed young woman crawls out.

"Please help him," she says. "I couldn't get him to talk to me."

Gwen and I release the man's seatbelt and ease him out through the passenger side. He's got a nasty contusion on his forehead and his left shoulder appears to be dislocated. Gwen decides not to pull it back in place because of the trauma. We can't call an ambulance—cell phones won't work out here—so we get him in the back of the 4Runner and take him to the clinic, where Gwen gives him what treatment she can. Then she calls Benefis Hospital in Great Falls to tell them we're bringing a patient in the ambulance.

While Gwen tends to the man in the back, his wife, April, tells me they left Des Moines last week for a backcountry skiing jaunt in the Rockies. They were coming down from East Glacier, trying to make it to Lincoln, where they had motel reservations, when a truck careened around a curve onto their side of the road as they descended the hill near the gravel pit. The husband wrenched the wheel to get out of the truck's path. April thought the Explorer had turned over three times before it landed at the bottom of the gulley.

By the time we get to Great Falls, the man has just begun to regain consciousness. He has a concussion and a dislocated shoulder but no broken bones. The doctors want to keep him overnight for observation. April has only bruises and minor cuts. The doctor prescribes a sedative, and before Gwen and I leave for home, we take her to a motel, tell her to call her insurance company in the morning, and write down our phone numbers in case she needs more help. Then we go to the state police headquarters to report the accident and tell them about the kids in the GMC truck.

"We had a report on them two hours ago," an officer tells us. "They went through Guthrie doing about sixty. The town police called one of our cruisers. He followed them up 89. They wiped out on that bridge up at Dupuyer Creek. Bob Nance said there were bodies all over the place. Two of the kids survived the crash, but neither is expected to live.

"There'll be a new row of white crosses at that bridge next week. Lord, how many are there on Route 89 now! Damned Indian kids—alcohol and gasoline—it's a deadly mixture."

He asks if the couple is going to be all right and says he'll send someone to the hospital in the morning to get a report, and a wrecker to see if anything can be done with their car.

"If they need any help, you can call us," I say, and give him my card.

"We will. You betcha. But we'll try to make sure they're taken care of."

When we get back to Clark City at four in the morning, we're exhausted. We stop by Gwen's apartment to get Spook, then drive over to my bungalow and go straight to bed. When I wake, the eastern horizon is just beginning to lighten. Gwen is curled close against me. I tighten my arm around her. She is sobbing quietly into my shoulder.

Chapter Seven

IT'S HALF PAST NOON BY THE TIME WE FINISH BREAKFAST. GWEN HAS taken Spook for a long walk, so I call the sheriff's office in Helena. Ralston isn't there. I ask if I can have his home number.

"I'm sorry, Mr. Battle," the voice on the other end replies, "but we're not allowed to give that out. But if it's important, I can call him and he can call you."

"It's important."

Forty-five minutes later, Ralston calls. I start to tell him what I learned from Jeremy, but he interrupts to ask if I can come into town. He'd rather not talk about it on the phone. Is he afraid he's tapped? That I'm tapped? I'm beginning to get paranoid about everything myself.

"I never know about that phone," he says when I get to his office. "Yours could be tapped, you know. Probably not, but there are some other things I need to talk with you about in person. There are too many possibilities in this case."

"Not as many as there were yesterday morning."

"What do you mean?"

I tell him what Jeremy told me.

"Lord, Jake. You're a furlong ahead of me. Who is this big ugly guy? I haven't even heard about him."

"I don't know who he is, but it's a cinch he's the killer. And I don't know how to find out who he is without asking Buck. And asking Buck is going to put Jeremy and Olivia in danger. You can't put Buck in jail without any evidence."

"You're right. Turrentine let us search Mrs. Turrentine's rooms last week. We looked all around the place and didn't find anything suspicious. If she was using dope, we didn't find it. Maybe Turrentine cleaned the place up before we got there."

He drums his knuckles on the desk.

"Jake, I don't want you to put yourself in danger, but I know you won't keep your nose out of things no matter what I say. I'm a hundred miles from Clark City and I'm understaffed. Maybe the best thing for me to do is deputize you. . . . You got a gun?"

"I've got a Uberti .44-40 lever action and a Sako .30-06."

"No, I mean a pistol."

"I have a Sauer .44 Magnum Western Marshal."

He shakes his head. "That's too big to lug around. I'm going to issue you an M&P .38 special. You got a shotgun?"

"A Browning semiautomatic 12 gauge."

"Well, I want you to put that .30-06 and the shotgun—take the plug out—in your truck whenever you leave home. Don't keep them in the rack. Hide them in the backseat, and keep the .38 handy wherever you are.

"I know you're a sane man," Ralston says, hunting around his office for a shoulder harness to lend me so I can keep the revolver under my jacket. "I know you saw a lot of action in Vietnam. And I know you won't use that firepower unless you have to. But you might have to. If things start popping out there, it'll take me over an hour to get to Clark City. Another twenty minutes to the Turrentines' place. You're going to have to fill in for me until I get there."

Ralston goes through the motions of swearing me in. Then he gets the .38 special, and after I strap on the shoulder holster, he hands me three boxes of ammunition. Then he gives me two pair of handcuffs with keys and his home phone number.

"Stop by the road on the way back and shoot it a few times to get the feel of it," he says.

I am surprised that Ralston is deputizing me, but he's right: I'm not going to keep my nose out of the case. I'm also pleased to have the authority to protect Clark City if Buck Wallace or, particularly, the Goon puts us in danger.

"Ralston, if you call Buck and ask him when he expects Turrentine back, he won't think that's unusual. I'm afraid if I ask him, he'll get the wind up, but I don't think we can move forward on this case until Turrentine gets back . . . unless the big guy shows his face again."

"We may even have to call Turrentine and tell him we need him here. I can do that. I'll find out from Buck how to get in touch. You betcha."

Outside I find snow drifting down through the streetlights again, the first in over a week. It's nearly seven o'clock, so I go down to the Lewis & Clark Hotel for dinner. Wilson is in a good head. He pours me a half-tumbler of Glenmorangie Claret Wood and tells me about the game he's been watching between the Lions and Broncos. Wilson can't decide whether to be a Denver or Seattle fan. I bet him whenever either of them is playing the Redskins, and usually lose.

He says he has a good idea for my novel.

"When that guy—what's his name—George? When George gets caught down there on Yellowstone Lake, why don't you have a wolverine raid his camp? Make it real scary. Didn't you tell me it was a wolverine that dug up Mrs. Turrentine? Lord, I'm glad I didn't have to see that. Them damned wolverines, it's like they're from some other dimension. . . . You want another Glenmorangie? Looks like you need some more nectar from the valley of tranquility."

After my dinner—a small rack of lamb with an excellent mint glaze and rosemary sprigs, steamed baby carrots, and green peas—I decide to spend the night in Helena. I call Gwen to let her know, then go back in the bar and have a Grand Marnier with Wilson; he puts his glass on the shelf behind the bar and takes sips when no one is looking. We talk football for a while, then I go up to bed. But not to sleep—my mind starts off one way, then it veers another. One thing that's been bothering me the last two days is Jeremy's story. I keep imagining what it must have been like to watch helplessly as someone ends your career by cutting across your hands with a straight razor. All I can feel is a dreadful queasiness in my stomach.

Then my mind jumps to Bat, or whatever his name is. Obviously he, Lila, and Buck were in the dope business. I'm guessing Bat was flying the stuff in from Mexico or maybe Guatemala, then Lila and Buck were delivering it to some dealer in Great Falls or Helena or Butte. But where did the guy come from, and how did Lila get hooked up with him? From what Jeremy told me, I guess Lila brought Buck into the business—she'd have had to. But why the big argument, and why did they go out to Golden Meadows? It seems like Lila went there willingly. May even have been the one who instigated the ride. And how did Buck play into all of this? Where was he when Lila was shot? I guess I'll have to get those answers from Buck himself. But how?

My mind works its way around to a story my cousin, Joe Pete, once told me. He owned Burnt Quarter, an old plantation over in Dinwiddie County, Virginia. The place had been in his family nearly three hundred years. One Sunday afternoon he was napping on the back porch after a couple of drinks, half asleep, he said, when suddenly the smokehouse, about fifty yards down toward the old slave quarter, exploded.

"Just exploded," he said. "A real bona fide explosion. Almost knocked me out of my chair."

The roof lifted off intact until it was fifteen feet or so in the air, then the tin twisted into a snarl around the rafters and darted off down the hill. The walls flew apart: boards and posts, beams and studs, hams and shoulders, sides of bacon and slabs of fatback were hurled helter-skelter in all directions.

"It was weird," he told me, "watching all that lumber and meat flying through the air, like in slow motion. Like it had all suddenly come to life and was performing some ritual dance, graceful but macabre, before it gave up its life and fell back to earth."

Before he could get out of his rocker and down the steps, everything had settled except the dust. He never did quite figure out what had happened. They'd smoked the meat three weeks before. The smokehouse itself was a hundred or more years old. Maybe a spark from the hickory fire had gotten into the floor, which was soaked with the fat of more than a hundred years of curings. Maybe it had smoldered there for a few weeks, working its way through cracks and veins in the wood until a flashpoint was reached. And then suddenly–*boom!* Joe Pete had to depend on his neighbors for good home-cured hog meat that year.

Joe Pete could tell that story. He had told it so many times he had every word and nuance in place. And he had a few dozen other ones as well. I lie there chuckling as I give in to sleep. Back home everyone misses you, Old Joe Pete. . . .

Chapter Eight

TONIGHT WHEN I WALK INTO JODY'S, GUS FOX SHOUTS AT ME FROM across the room.

"Hey, fellow, we don't allow anybody in here unless they're wearing cowboy boots—particularly if he's a lawman."

Gus is the resident wiseacre, convivial drinker, and good humor man. He's also one of the best nature photographers in the country, with a couple of impressive coffee table books published by an outfit in Minneapolis.

"I left my boots down at the stable," I call back. "They had manure halfway up the shafts. Unfit for genteel Clark City company, and what do you mean, 'lawman?' "

"You forget that Sheriff Nichols deputized you yesterday?"

"No, but how did you know?"

"He called out this morning and told Eva Gertrude at the post office in case there were any questions about it."

I sit down with Gus and his buddy, Bill Williams, the foreman on the Lazy L, one of the smaller spreads north of town, and order a drink.

"So I guess you're the new gun in Clark City. Tell me if you plan to have a showdown with anybody," Gus says. "Give me enough time to get out of town. I don't want to get caught by a stray bullet."

They ask what's going on in the murder case. I tell them Ralston is baffled. Carlton is still a suspect but not a very likely one. Ralston is waiting for something to break.

"What about you, Jake?" Gus asks. "You got any ideas?"

"No," I tell them. "But I'm pretty sure Carlton couldn't have killed her. That's all I know now."

We talk for a while about the lousy elk season this year. Then about the weather. Then who's going to be matched up in the NFL playoffs. When I finish my drink, I decide to walk down to the Antler to see if Carlton is imbibing his nightly potions. He's not there, but Tim Free has got Wilbur Watt backed into a corner and is giving him hell.

"You goddamn pussy-snappers. What the fuck did you think you were doing? Those elk out there are sacred. Sacred! Without them what would this place be? Fifty years ago there was hardly any elk left on this side of the divide. That's why they created the preserve. All of us in the business agreed not to take any more elk than is healthy for the herd. You agreed to that, you lipless cocksucker. . . ."

Tim is a little plug of a fellow, about five foot seven, a hundred eighty pounds. He's Gus Fox's half brother and about the most foul-mouthed man I've ever known. He'll tell the most obscene jokes no matter who's listening: women, preachers, pillars of the community—but not kids, thank God. He also says whatever he thinks, without inhibition or consideration for feelings. Consequently, some of the locals don't like him, but Tim has got the right values and a heart as big as a watermelon. He and Carlton work together a lot on construction and carpentry projects. And Tim is also a hunting and fishing guide during the seasons.

Wilbur, who's a prosperous outfitter and guide, was mixed up in a nefarious scheme of the Fish and Wildlife people to curry favor with some state and federal politicians back in October. One of the F&W patrol helicopters was used to herd a large band of elk off the Sun River Game Preserve out onto the open hills near Sawtooth Ridge. Wilbur and some of the F&W people had transported the politicians in four-wheel-drive pickups for what amounted to target practice on living animals—a real slaughter. Many of the elk were shot from the moving vehicles. Nearly every law and rule of hunting decency was broken to satisfy the bloodlust of the politicians and solicit their votes for budgetary allocations to the Fish and Wildlife Department.

"What's going to be left for us to guide people in for? What's going to be left for our children if you hen-diddling sons of bitches fling shit like that in the faces of law-abiding sportsmen. Those Fish and Wildlife people are a bunch of ass-licking creepy crawlers anyway. They ought to be dropped in a shit hole and then strung up by their balls—you along with them. . . ."

Wilbur has been near speechless through the whole tirade, his weak attempts to protest squashed by more volleys from Tim. I listen to the harangue until Tim exhausts his rather impressive, if limited, vocabulary.

"Fuck you peckerless sphincter smoochers anyway," is his parting shot at Wilbur, before stomping off.

At last left alone with a couple of friends at the far end of the bar, Wilbur tries to save face by calmly finishing his drink before nodding to his buddies that it's time to depart. But clearly he is badly shaken, and ostracized—everyone else has moved away, leaving him and his two buddies isolated in their little corner. I guess it will be a long while before Wilbur comes back to the Antler to socialize.

Phil Turner, the owner of the bar, has seemed rather amused by the diatribe, probably happy to have Tim articulate the general feeling of the hunting community. Now he and Tim are talking at the other end of the bar, and I watch Tim moderate from a rolling boil to a simmer and then to room temperature. In a few minutes he's back to telling jokes.

"Hey, Jake," he calls from his end of the bar. "Why are cowgirls bowlegged?"

"I don't know, Tim. Why are cowgirls bowlegged?"

"Because cowboys eat with their hats on. You want to borrow my hat? Gwen is awfully straight-legged for a cowgirl."

Everybody has a good laugh at my expense, which is all right by me.

About that time, Carlton bursts through the door. He's a little wild-eyed when he comes over and nudges me away from the crowd.

"Jake, I think I saw the big guy that Wilson Toliver and Gwen told you about."

He says the man was driving Lila's Land Rover out on Simms Road, headed east.

"It was about two-thirty, so I got a good look. I never seen him before, but I could tell he was tall, even sitting down. And ugly—his face was put together at all the wrong angles."

Carlton had turned around to follow the guy but couldn't keep up in his old Toyota pickup. He'd gone on into Great Falls anyway and driven around for a couple of hours trying to spot the Land Rover.

"Even went out to the airport, but I couldn't find him. Maybe he took the interstate on up into Canada."

I hustle Carlton outside and walk him over to my bungalow, telling him on the way what I'd learned from Jeremy and about Ralston deputizing me.

"*I-yuke,* kemo sabe, you've sort of out-galloped me. Is Ralston satisfied now that I didn't kill Lila?"

"He didn't ever think you did. It was just the D.A. wanted to make quick work of the case to impress Turrentine."

"Well, Mr. Deputy, whenever you need my services for a posse, I'm available. I'd like to be the one that gets that son of a bitch. I'd like to get Buck Wallace too. That guy has always given me a hard time. I could tell he was really upset when he realized I was getting into Lila's riding breeches. He'd probably have tried to beat my ass if she hadn't been his meal ticket."

I give Carlton a drink—he likes Black Jack Daniel's but can't afford to buy it at the bars, so I keep a bottle for his visits. Next I call Ralston at home and tell him what Carlton saw.

"Hell of a time of night to be calling in, Jake. But that's okay. I'll have Barney look up the license number and put out an APB to pick him up. He's probably hell-bent for Canada though."

Ralston promises to call me back tomorrow if anything breaks.

When I hang up, Carlton asks, "Why don't Ralston go ahead and arrest Buck? Jeremy could testify against him."

"Testify to what? That he saw him in company with Lila and the monster? There's really no evidence against him. Ralston couldn't even find any dope out there."

"What I wonder is how that big guy got ahold of my rifle. That's what baffles me. I asked Bob if he saw any strangers hanging around the Bunkhouse near the time Lila was shot. He said nobody but the clientele and visitors like you. People he knows."

It's nearly midnight. I pour Carlton another drink and tell him it's the last one, then I call Gwen, though she hates to be awakened after she's gone to bed. The phone rings four times, then the answering machine switches on.

"Gwen," I say.

She picks up the phone.

"What the hell, Jake? I've got to work tomorrow, and, no, I'm not going to hump over to your place tonight."

"Carlton saw that big ugly guy today on the way to Great Falls in Lila's Land Rover. He's around and God knows what he's up to. You keep your eyes peeled for him tomorrow. If you see him, give me a call immediately. You're one of the few people who's seen him before."

"Okay, sorry I flew off the handle. I missed you today. Eva Gertrude told me Ralston deputized you. I hope you're not going to use your newly acquired power to abuse me. . . . On second thought—"

"Go back to sleep. I'm dead tired. I'm going to bed as soon as I can chase Carlton out of the house."

Lying in bed, I try to form a mental picture of what this guy Bat looks like from the vague descriptions I've gotten from Gwen, Wilson, Carlton, and Jeremy, who compared him to the guy in the James Bond flicks. In my weary mind, he begins to look like creatures from *Night of the Living Dead*. Then Nosferatu. Then he metamorphoses into Victor Frankenstein's monster. Finally I see him leering at me from the bathroom mirror. I'm startled, wondering how that could be. But beneath the haphazard planes of his face, I see my eyes, my nose, my mouth. I get up and mix warmed milk with a big slug of Myers's Rum and drink it all down before I go back to bed.

Chapter Nine

THIS MORNING WHEN I GO OUT TO GET THE NEWSPAPER FROM THE front porch, I notice a letter sticking up in my mailbox. It hadn't been there when I got home last night. The plain business envelope is addressed in block letters written with a No. 2B pencil to Dr. Jacob Carter Battle—no street address, no city, no state, no zip code. No stamp either. After I pour my coffee, I rip open the envelope and look inside: one sheet of plain white paper. In the center of the sheet are pasted letters and words obviously cut from a magazine:

http://www.darlasplayground.com
Click on gallery six. Click on set nine.

And that's all. I ponder the two lines for a minute before it dawns on me that it's a Web address for a porn site. I wonder why anyone would send me surfing for pornography. I get email solicitations from time to time, but this is clearly hand-delivered and local.

After breakfast I hook up my PowerBook and leap onto the Web, wondering whether I'm the spider or the prey. Darla's Playground requires a $4.95 trial membership fee so I go in the bedroom and get my VISA card, thinking how twenty-five years ago if somebody had told me I could get most anything I wanted over a telephone line with electronic money, I would have thought he was crazy. When I connect to the members' page, naked women are all over the screen in various poses and situations. *Gallery 6, Set 9* reveals a sequence of thumbnails striping down the left side of the screen. All I can tell is that there are two women in various positions of intimacy. When I enlarge the first picture, it takes me a full ten seconds to realize that one of the women is a very youthful Lila. She and a beautiful redhead are standing skimpily clad, holding each other, breasts and bellies pressed together, looking intently into each other's eyes. On the wall behind them hangs a copy of Courbet's *The Sleepers*. In the second picture Lila and the redhead are half undressed, their breasts bared, kissing passionately. In the next picture they are entirely undressed, sitting on the edge of an enormous satin-covered bed. Again they are kissing, and the redhead has her hand between Lila's thighs. By the time I get to picture ten, they have been through all manner of caresses, breast sucklings, and belly kissing. Lila is lying back on the bed with the redhead between her legs licking her sex. This is no suggestive feigning; the woman's tongue is vigorously buried in Lila's vulva. By picture twelve the positions are reversed. And by picture fifteen they are in a mutual embrace popularly known as a 69. In the last picture, number sixteen, they are lying side by side, kissing affectionately.

These are no sleazy, cheaply made pictures. The women are beautiful, their sensual energy is convincingly urgent, the setting is elegant, and the picture quality is of the highest standard, seemingly taken, although there are no credits, by a professional glamour photographer. But why on earth would Lila have made them? From what I knew of her life, she would never have needed money badly. But then she didn't need the money she would have gotten from running cocaine either. Was it for kicks? She and the redhead sure looked as if they were enjoying each other. Here in Montana she had made the rounds of beds, and from what I'd heard, in Houston as well. Probably in New York and Hollywood too.

I think of Marilyn Monroe, Grace Kelly, Carroll Baker—what drove those women to their promiscuity? Excitement? The need for adulation? A sense of power? Or maybe just to assert one's free agency. In the pictures Lila doesn't look as if she could have been more than twenty or twenty-one years old. That would have been about the time she left Sweet Briar and moved to New York. I wonder if Randal Turrentine knows about these pictures. Someone—Ralston or I—will have to ask him. What do they tell us about Lila? Who wanted me to see these pictures enough to leave a surreptitious and anonymous note in my box? More questions. More mystery. More gutter filth. Yet I have to admit that beyond my initial astonishment, I'm excited by the photographs. I go back through the sequence. Then I save them on my hard drive. When I get up to go to the bathroom, I'm so aroused I can't piss.

When I was wounded in Vietnam, I was evacuated express to Japan. The medical people were always afraid that any mine or booby trap Charlie set was smeared with shit, thus the possibility of deadly infection and gangrene. They kept me in the hospital at Kishine Barracks in Yokohama for nearly a month, cleaning my wound, bandaging my burns, and shooting me up with antibiotics. When I was released, the unit C.O. asked if I'd like two weeks of R&R in Bangkok before reporting back for combat duty. They set me up with hotel reservations, gave me guidebooks and a pamphlet with handy Thai phrases, V.D. warnings, a box of rubbers—the usual military indoctrination packet for foreign places. In Bangkok I ran into an old acquaintance from OCS who was staying in the same hotel. He had been there for nearly two weeks and had found all the "good places." He took me to a dive down in the Patpong district where there were lots of bar girls, but the main attraction was exotic dancing. Each dancer had her own specialty: one was a contortionist whose tongue caressed her most intimate parts, another demonstrated how to snuff a flaming baton, one picked up silver dollars with her labia. At the end of a couple of hours, both of us had girls sitting on our laps, kneading our crotches, slurping their watered down "champagne cocktails" as fast as we could buy them. I didn't particularly like mine—she was trim and good-looking enough, but there was an odd smell about her. I wanted to get rid of her but didn't know how. Then this dancer comes on-

stage. She was a real knockout, tall for a Thai, about five foot seven. She dances around with a great deal of sensuality, doing ballet-quality movements. She doesn't seem to have any tricks, but the audience is obviously interested, urging her on. Finally, a native guy over near the bar tosses her a liqueur bottle, the long-necked kind Strega and some kinds of sake come in. She places the bottle center stage and makes up to it, dancing around it suggestively like it's some partner to be won. Then she dances over it and slowly lowers herself onto the neck. I'd guess about eight inches gets up inside her before she lifts it off the floor and begins to move her hips, very slowly at first. The bottle begins to make pendular, then circular movements. She has it under absolute control, like a precocious twelve-year-old with a hula hoop. Her movements become more energetic. The bottle is swirling up and then back, making figure eights. The amazing thing is that it doesn't fly out of her. She starts a series of long, smooth forward and backward motions, swinging the bottle higher and higher. Her eyes survey the crowd, lingering a moment here, a moment there. For about ten seconds she fixes on me and smiles before turning back toward the bar. Then, as the music reaches its climax, she makes a sudden thrust with her pelvis and releases the bottle so that it flies in a high arc over the heads of the audience and is caught by the man at the bar who had thrown it to her. He licks the neck slowly and smiles. The audience goes bananas. They give her a wild ovation, shouting, "Nittaya! Nittaya!" She bows and exits the stage. Ten minutes later I am still trying to figure out how I can get rid of the girl on my lap when Nittaya comes out from behind the stage fully dressed. She walks over to our table and says something to the girl sitting in my lap. The girl frowns but gets up and walks over to the bar. Nittaya swings a chair from the next table over beside me and sits down.

"Buy me drink?" she says.

"Sure."

She orders a vodka and tonic, with real Ukraine vodka. One for me too.

"You here from Vietnam?"

I tell her about my wound and the R&R. She drinks her vodka and looks hard at me. Her eyes are very black.

"It dirty war. What you want fight the Minh for? You get killed," she says.

"It wasn't my idea. Uncle Sam enlisted my services and provided transportation. I'd as soon be back in the States."

We talk for a while, but the language barrier is difficult. When she asks if I've been with a Thai girl yet, I say no, I just got in yesterday.

"You like come with me?"

"Sure. Where are we going?"

She reaches over and takes my hand.

"Let go," she says. "Come on. Let go."

Suddenly we are in the street, hurrying along through the pedestrian, bike, and motor traffic. Soon we are out of the Patpong district into an area of respectable apartments and townhouses. She pulls me into a building and punches a code into a keypad near the elevator. We get off on the ninth floor. Her apartment is not elegant, but it is exotic, crammed full of glass and pottery pieces, mats and curtains, pictures in bamboo frames, and Hindu relief sculptures. Two birds flap around in a cage and a pale submarine glow ebbs from a small aquarium. We take off our shoes, then she leads me through an archway into her bedroom. She hasn't spoken since we left the club. Now she says, "Come, take off clothes." She doesn't wait for me to respond, but begins to unbutton my shirt, unbuckle my belt, rip down my shorts. She "smokes" me; my penis is so rigid when she takes it out of her mouth that I think it might take leave of my body. She slips out of her dress—she isn't wearing anything under it—and pulls me down on the bed.

"Let go! Pom Pom! Let go!"

I had never spent such an erotic night in my life. And haven't since. She made sure it wasn't just about physical gratification. She was here, she was there, leading, urging. By morning I could have been laid in a coffin and nobody would have suspected I was alive. At noon she woke me and fed me food she'd brought in from a local restaurant. When I got ready to leave, I reached for my wallet and took out two thousand bhat to pay her.

"No! No! Shan shob khun. *Wit you I not whore!" she says with a great deal of emphasis and disgust. "Tonight. You come to Ishtar Hide'way tonight. Don't let no girl sit on yo lap."*

It's like a dream. For the next ten days, it's the same thing—every night. I am getting so worn down I wonder if I won't get sent back to the hospital when I report for duty at the end of the next week. Nittaya must think my exhaustion is a sign of waning interest. Each night she tries new tricks. Each night I respond but flag before she is ready to bring our lovemaking to an end. Two nights before I'm to fly back to Saigon, she introduces a new excitement. When we leave Ishtar's Hideaway, we don't go straight to her apartment. First we go to another club two blocks away. We drink Singha and watch the dancers. I am wondering what's going on until one of the girls comes out from behind the stage and walks over to our table. Nittaya stands up and embraces her, then takes the girl's arm and turns her toward me.

"Onuma," she says.

Onuma smiles and does a half bow. Soon the three of us are in Nittaya's apartment, where she hands me a drink and directs me to sit on a short stool near her bed. She and Onuma begin a performance—or maybe it's not a performance. They undress and caress each other. They kiss. They lie on the bed entangled. They go through every position imaginable. At first I'm so stunned that I don't respond sexually. I drink from the glass compulsively. But soon I'm so excited that I'm feeling myself through my tight pants, ready to enter the frolic, but they seem to be in no hurry. I waste myself, blotching one pant leg, though when Nittaya motions for me to join them, I am ready again.

Next morning Nittaya sends Onuma away. I don't go back to my hotel. Nittaya doesn't go to work that night. The next day, when I have to rush back to my room and pack for the plane, she comes with me. At the airport she kisses me. She doesn't weep. She doesn't smile.

"Yankee sojer, don't let no Minh bullet kill you," she says, before turning and walking away, back to the concourse and the taxi that is waiting to take her to Ishtar's Hideaway.

Sometimes I try to imagine her today. I wonder if she is still alive. She would certainly be too old to dance, or even to be a bar girl. Whatever happens to those people anyway?

Around ten-thirty Ralston calls me. The airport police in Butte found the Land Rover in a fifteen-minute parking space. A search of the terminal turned up no one fitting the monster's description. Presently the city police are questioning terminal personnel and taxi drivers and checking ticket sales and car rentals to see if there might be a lead somewhere. They also are checking to see if he flew out in a private plane.

"Looks like a dead end, Jake. I'm sure the guy knew we'd be looking for the Land Rover and ditched it. Them damned drug runners develop this early warning system when they're being followed or put under surveillance."

I tell him about the Lila porno pictures.

"Lord, Jake, how do you get onto all this stuff? You think they could have anything to do with the murder?"

"I doubt it. But who knows. We'll have to ask Turrentine about them if he ever gets back. You have any luck locating him?"

"No. He wasn't at the El Paso number Buck Wallace gave me. I've got a call in to his Houston office. I'm sure they know where he is, but they haven't called me back."

I ask him where he wants me to send the Lila pictures, his office or his home.

"Home," he says and gives me his email address.

I call Gwen to make a date for tonight, but she has a medical meeting this afternoon in Great Falls and won't get home until late tonight, so I decide to work on the novel. My hero is on a quest to find and kill a great white buffalo in what are called the Sweet Grass Hills northeast of present-day Shelby. He's not having much luck finding the beast, and I'm not having much luck getting the episode to flow. I stop for lunch, then plug on through the afternoon. By six, I have about five hundred words written. Next session I'll probably throw them away and start all over. But that's the way writing goes. At least I've internalized a few ideas. Maybe the episode will start writing itself.

Chapter Ten

TEN MORE DAYS UNTIL CHRISTMAS. THIS MORNING I CALL DOWN TO Twin Bridges to see if R.L. Winston has any of their new Joan Wulff 4-weight rods in stock. I've decided to give Gwen one for Christmas. She's an avid fly fisherman; that was one of the interests that first attracted us to each other. After I'd driven the ambulance for her a few times and taken her to dinner, I found out how much she liked fishing, so I invited her on a four-day trip up the North Fork of the Sun.

"The rainbows up there are big fighters," I told her. "It'll be a nice backpack."

"Backpack! Why don't we take my horse? I'll borrow one for you from Lacy Andrews."

"No exercise. Just flattens your ass. Backpacking . . . that's the way to stay in shape. Tightens your buttocks. Trims your waist. Sharpens your sex drive. When you're my age, you need all the backpacking you can get. Besides, I'll carry most of the weight."

That convinced her.

The fishing was wonderful. It was high August and the prairies and hills were luscious green, the water level just right. We caught and ate lots of fish. Bathed naked in the river. Made love wherever and whenever we wanted It was there we decided that we were a couple. Marriage? Well, we'd wait and see about that.

She uses an old 9-foot HMG 6-weight. Had been for years. It

caught plenty of fish, but casting was a labor. I decided she should be rewarded with an elegant rod—and if there's anyone who makes an elegant rod, it's R.L.Winston. A couple of years ago the company asked Joan Wulff to design one especially for women, and she did: The grip is smaller and shaped to fit a woman's hand. When I call, the lady at Winston says they have four on display in the showroom.

I call Ralston to tell him I'm going to Twin Bridges and ask if the Butte police have turned up any trace of the Goon.

"They think he may have rented a car from Budget. I wasn't here when they called. Barney wasn't clear about the message—you know how he is."

Ralston asks me to stop by the police station down there since it's on my way and see what they've found. The D.A. has him completely tied up working a robbery yesterday at a Montana First branch just outside the city limits, outside Helena police jurisdiction.

"A lousy break for me," Ralston says. "Lots of public squawking. You'll have to carry the load on this Turrentine case for a while."

He tells me to keep an expense account and that he'll get me reimbursed.

"Sorry I can't pay you a salary, Jake. But I know you are a dutiful citizen."

I say okay and call Gwen to tell her I'm going to Butte and won't be back until late tonight.

"They found Lila's Land Rover down there at the airport. Nobody knows where the Goon is though."

"You guys need to get this Lila thing solved, else it's going to ruin our sex life. . . . What we need is to go fishing . . . get away from all this evil. But since I've got to work tomorrow, why don't you come over to my apartment tomorrow night? I'll cook you a gourmet feast. Then we can see what happens afterward."

I'm happy to be out in the 4Runner by myself. Zipping along these Montana roads with almost no traffic gives me a chance to clear my head. I survey the brown and gray hills slumbering in the wan winter sunlight, conserving their energies, preparing for their springtime effusions in four or five months. I slip in a tape of Mozart's *Sinfonia Concertante* and head down U.S. 287 until it intersects the interstate, then down I-15 through Helena to Boulder, across the all-weather road to Whitehall, then down 55 to Twin Bridges. Along the way I let Mozart's logical clarity reorganize my brain and try to answer my growing list of questions:

Q) Where did Lila meet the ugly guy—this Goon?

A) With no facts, I have to guess: To satisfy her coke habit, she needed a contact, a source. Probably in Great Falls, since it's closer to Clark City than Helena, and bigger. Also, it has an air base, i.e., transient military personnel. Goon is probably a dealer or a supplier of a dealer. He finds out she has an airstrip on a remote ranch in Ordway County at her disposal, and proposes a deal. Or maybe there's a dealer who buys his stuff from Goon. When the dealer finds out Lila has access to a private airstrip, he negotiates an arrangement involving Lila and Goon. What we need to do is locate the dealer in Great Falls and see if we can find out who and where Goon is. I have no contacts, so Ralston will have to do that.

Q) How did Goon get Carlton's rifle?

A) Goon would not have known about the rifle, but Buck Wallace had been around Clark City long enough to hear all the hunting stories. He came into the Antler regularly. Why would he want to steal the rifle? He's jealous when he finds out Carlton is screwing Lila. Maybe he's been privileged in her bed himself in the past but is now excluded. Somehow I doubt Lila would lower herself to that level, unless he was merely a stopgap between affairs. Nevertheless, Buck wants revenge on Carlton. One day he goes to the Bunkhouse when Carlton is out working on the barn at the Circle 9. He waits for Bob to go on an errand, or go hunting, or go to Helena, then he slips into Carlton's room and takes the gun. Maybe he plans to shoot Carlton and make it look like an accident. Maybe he plans to shoot Lila and make it look like

Carlton did it. But he never gets the chance. He has the gun in his quarters out at the Circle 9, so when he learns that Goon is going out to Golden Meadows with Lila and wants a gun—something besides a pistol or a shotgun—Buck lends him the .25-35 Winchester?

Q) Who fired the two rounds from a .32 out at Golden Meadows? And why?

A) Lila? Did she have a .32? That I'll have to find out from Randal. Was she protecting herself from Goon? Was she trying to kill Goon because he was making big trouble for her? Did she shoot first and incite Goon to kill her?

Q) Where was Buck when the shooting took place?

A) Probably not at Golden Meadows. Carlton saw only the two sets of horse prints. Was Buck waiting for Goon and Lila at the horse trailer? Where would that have been? At Mortimer Gulch? At Benchmark? The two trailheads are about equal distance from Golden Meadows.

Q) Why didn't Buck come back with Goon to the Circle 9 on Monday?

A) He wasn't at the trailer but had gone somewhere on other business. Or Lila had told him (or he had intuited) that she intended to kill Goon. But when Goon came back without her, Buck got scared and fled in the Yukon.

Q) The big question here: Why would Lila have wanted to kill Goon?

A) Maybe he had become a threat to her. But I don't know enough to make an intelligent guess. Only Goon or Buck would know.

Q) Why did Lila take Goon out to Golden Meadows in the first place? What reason did she give him?

A) I haven't the foggiest.

Q) Who put the letter about Darla's Playground in my mailbox?

A) An interesting question. Who would have benefited from it? Not Turrentine, certainly. Besides, he wasn't in town. Not Buck: he probably doesn't even know how to operate a computer. My guess is that it was some townsperson who just stumbled on the pictures surfing the net. But who? There was some jocular speculation around town that Billy Nims, who works part-time at the post office with Eva Gertrude, is a porn surfer. He could have run across the pictures, and knowing I was involved with the case and was now deputized, sneaked the letter into my mailbox. He would probably have been afraid to deliver the address directly to Ralston. And like everyone else, he's probably watched enough television to pick up the idea of cutting out words and letters from a magazine rather than writing them out by hand or on a typewriter.

Q) Finally, why am I so deeply involved in this fucking case?

A) One—I'm fascinated by Lila? Two—Fate: I found her body? Three—I'm too bloody stupid to kiss the case goodbye and let Ralston do his job?

Evelyn, an all-purpose admin assistant and rod expert at the R.L. Winston factory, shows me the four rods.

"Look them over carefully. There are minor differences, since each one is hand built. See, the cork on this one is a different color from the others. This one here we made with an uplocking reel seat, rather than the normal downlocking, which Joan Wulff prefers. You can go out back and cast each one if you want. I'll get you a reel with a four-weight line."

I tell her that won't be necessary, but I would like to put each one together and lock on a reel to see how it feels—which I do. I flick each one up and down to make the rod oscillate to get a feel for the action. They all feel about the same, but the uplocking rod has a slightly different balance that I like. I look over the work carefully, admiring the meticulous detail, the deep green color, the smoothness of the sanding, the exact fit of the ferrules, the perfect winding on each guide. It's one of the handsomest graphite rods I've ever seen. I tell Evelyn that I'll take it.

"You betcha, I like that one too," she says. "Since you drove all the way down from Clark City, I'm giving you a 15 percent discount. That will save you about eighty-five dollars. . . ."

She gives me a friendly smile.

"I also like the idea you're giving it as a Christmas present to your lady."

On the way up to Butte, I intend to have another question-answer session, but the beautiful rod in its case on the seat next to me has me too excited to concentrate. Visions of future fishing trips with Gwen dance through my head. When I pull up in front of the police station in Butte, Lila's murder has receded to some distant chamber of my mind. I mentally ratchet my brain around until I get back on track, then I go inside, where Lew Durham, an assistant to the chief, leads me into a conference room.

"Sheriff Nichols called to tell us you were coming, Mr. Battle. . . . Here's what we have. We believe the man you are looking for is named Dimitri Ivanovich Sulamanov. At least that's the name he gave when he rented the car—a 1998 Montero. The car has already been turned in at Great Falls, so that's not going to help us. But we pulled fingerprints off the door and steering wheel of the Land Rover belonging to Mrs. Turrentine and a James Henry Wallace–you might want to go over his record, which the Houston police faxed up to us. Great Falls is pulling the prints off the Montero. So far neither of us has an identification."

The car rental agent told Durham the man's driver's license appeared to be in order: The name matched the one he gave; the picture matched his face. The agent described the suspect as being very tall; she thought his license said six foot seven. His hair was a "washed-out brown," trimmed close but with a shock in front that fell down over his forehead. His license said his eyes were brown, but she hadn't looked closely: his face was so ugly it was frightening. She did notice that his eyes were deep set. His brow was abnormally heavy, and his chin was both broad and deep. His nose was also large, but his face didn't look like it was put together right. She told police it looked something like a sculpture by some

Frenchman whose name she couldn't remember. She couldn't remember what the license said but guessed his weight to be at least two hundred fifty pounds.

"The license was issued by the State of Illinois," Durham tells me, "but we've checked; they have no record of the license number nor of anyone by the name of Dimitri Sulamanov."

He gives me a copy of the report along with Buck's record. I read over both before I leave the station. The report is just a repeat of what Durham has told me. But Buck's record is more interesting. There was a short sentence in Mississippi for aggravated assault and manslaughter, a rap he could probably have beaten on a self-defense plea if it hadn't been related to racketeering. He served less than a year of a five-year term at Parchman before being paroled. Somebody had probably ladened a few influential pockets to spring him so soon. Evidently he'd kept clean for the full probation. But in 1986 he was picked up in Houston on a concealed weapons charge. The case was dismissed, however, when a license for the weapon indicating that it was to be used for security purposes at Club Diablo was produced by Randal Turrentine. Turns out Buck was working as a detective/bouncer at Turrentine's nightclub at the time. There is no record of violations since '86.

On the way back to Clark City I stop at the sheriff's complex in Helena to drop off copies of the two reports for Ralston, then I go to a nice little Thai restaurant that has opened downtown on Last Chance Gulch. The food is first-rate, but they don't have an alcoholic beverage license. I place my order for the Roast Duck Darling and walk down the street to the Wrangler Bar, where I buy two Sierra Pale Ales, since they don't have Singha. When I get back, the meal is ready. The vegetables and sauce are excellent, and the duck has been roasted just enough to get most of the fat out before it was stir-fried with the vegetables. The sauce has just the right tang. I never ate better in Bangkok. After the meal, I don't feel like driving, but I want to get back to Clark City tonight. So I jack up my resolve and wheel off into the night.

Just north of the intersection of U.S. 287 and Highway 200, there is a high hill far enough from all the clusters of electric lights to let starlight stream down unimpeded. Tonight is especially clear; the temperature is near zero, there is no wind, and the quarter moon has already set. I stop the 4Runner on the crest and walk around for a few minutes to get my blood flowing. Then I arch my back and look up at the firmament. I have always, since childhood, been fascinated by the stars. When I was six and seven and eight years old, my great aunt used to take us kids out on the lawn in front of her old family home, where we would lie on a blanket enumerating planets and figuring constellations. In the '60s when I was devouring book after book of science fiction, I would gaze out, wondering where extraterrestrial life might exist and dreaming of a day when I would build a spaceship to navigate the far reaches of the universe. Since then I have become attuned to a different kind of wonder in the heavens: the heart-gripping, light-pinned splendor of the night sky.

Tonight as I survey the heavens, a welcome tranquility settles around me. Far to the south just above the horizon is Orion, the great hunter. And there, higher, just to the west, are Atlas's daughters, the Pleiades, whom Orion pursues eternally in vain. I turn my gaze toward the east, find Leo first, and then, as I follow the elliptic southward, Cancer and Gemini, Taurus, and Aries. Tailing into the western horizon is Pisces. I look up a little higher; there is Pegasus, our great symbol of the imagination, soaring above all. Then suffering Andromeda, and Perseus, who has come to rescue her. I also think of his slaying of the Medusa. That was his great heroic feat. Medusa: the emblem of life in all its beauty and horror, on whom to look directly would petrify any mortal. Perseus's mirrored shield allowed him to subdue the Gorgon, whose death released the winged Pegasus. Perhaps, as the myth implies, the petrifying horror of life can be confronted only through the mediation of art. But beyond those myths are even greater mysteries. As I gaze into the black velvet waste between Castor and Polaris, I think of the impenetrable depths of darkness on the far side of the stars. What lies beyond the realm of the visible? Some dumbfounding secret that we shall never be made privy to—at least in this life? And is there another?

A dark chill seeps into my bones, sending me hustling back to the warmth of my car and on through the night to my snug bed in Clark City.

Chapter Eleven

THIS MORNING THERE'S AN EMAIL FROM DAVE LIEBERMAN AWAITING me:

Dear Jake,

The enclosure from Abe Isaacs at Rice should give you a pretty good idea of Turrentine's rise to riches. A fascinating piece of economic biography. I leave it to you to make of it what you can. I hope it helps in solving Mrs. Turrentine's murder, which seemed much on your mind when you were here.

Betty sends her love and urges me to urge you to bring Gwen over to see us sometime during the holidays. Stay for two or three days if you can. We think of you often.

Take care,
Dave

The report is lengthy and disjointed, so I will summarize and try to put the details into some kind of order. It begins with a caveat by Isaacs: "This report is a hurriedly put together synopsis gathered from numerous sources. The facts are accurate, based on verifiable evidence except where noted as hearsay; many of the suppositions are informed guesses. I might add, however, that I and one of my colleagues here at Rice are *the* authorities on Randal Turrentine's career. We have in the works a monograph on Turrentine as part of an analysis of Enron's corporate structure, which we hope to publish next summer in *Fowler's Financial Digest*, well before the presidential election. Please consider all information herein confidential. Some of it is undocumented and cannot be included in our published account. . . ."

Although Turrentine's initial fortune was built through wildcatting and oil speculation while he was located in Shreveport, there is vague, unconfirmed evidence that he was involved with racketeering in New Orleans, a probable source of the capital he needed for his legitimate business interests. Isaacs lists company profits over the period 1957–67, which show substantial income, and are a matter of public record. Turrentine's move to Houston in 1967 launched a period of diversified investments. His speculation in cotton and wheat brokerage and futures, aerospace technology, and Arabian-American oil, through Texaco, are certainly legitimate, with no opportunities for manipulation except for trading on inside information, which was most certainly available to him. In 1968 he invested heavily in the Monsanto Corporation, which was furnishing the U.S. government with large quantities of Agent Orange for strategic deforestation in Vietnam. Turrentine increased his investments in Monsanto during the 1990s when the company was experimenting with GMOs and successfully patenting their modified seed to be used in conjunction with their herbicide Roundup. His investments in savings and loan expansions after the Garn-sponsored deregulation in 1980 offered any number of opportunities for manipulation through stock trading and off-bleeding of capital through loans with bogus security. There is reason to believe that he was as culpable as Charles Keating, Neil Bush, James Fail, or any of the other principals involved, but there was insufficient evidence to indict him. His name was mentioned, however, at five sessions of the federal hearings on the scandal.

In 1975 he bought controlling interest in Teufelgewehr Manufacturing, a small arms producer in Argentina. The registered name of the company was changed to T&T Arms in 1976, and the operation was greatly expanded over the next decade: T&T began producing various assault rifles, light machine guns, semiautomatic handguns, grenade launchers, and machine pistols. In 1978 it began producing antipersonnel mines of the Claymore and Bouncing Betty types. The company's most successful weapon has been the T&T 100A—a near copy of the Russian AK-100 assault rifle. Various of T&T's weapons began showing up in the arsenals of several African countries—notably Somalia, Ethiopia, and Nigeria—and among insurgent groups in the Middle East. Contra forces in Nicaragua and Honduras during Reagan's administration were furnished with T&T 100As in large numbers. Isaacs' inference, based on hearsay, is that payment for the weapons was made in cocaine shipments from Costa Rica to south central Texas in Cessna 310s and 402-Bs, and DC-3s. The hearsay information is that specific.

Isaacs notes at this point that Turrentine had close ties with both the Nixon and Reagan administrations. He contributed heavily to Nixon's 1968 and 1972, Reagan's 1980 and 1984, and George Bush's 1988 and 1992 campaigns. His investments in Aramco just before the severe oil shortages of 1973–74 may have been linked to tips from oil interests in Texas, or from the federal government. Isaacs states here that this is only speculation, since he has no concrete or hearsay evidence on the subject. Turrentine's ownership of Club Diablo, his Houston nightclub, is one of his most perplexing investments. Why would anyone, Isaacs asks, who was in high finance—oil, automotive, electronics, computer software, aerospace—and particularly someone implicated in the smuggling of drugs and weapons, involve himself in a business that could only invite attention from local police as well as the FBI, IRS, ATF, and other federal agencies? Turrentine did, in fact, establish the financing and management of the club independent of his legitimate investments and connections. His earlier involvement with the rackets in New Orleans may account for what would seem to be aberrant economic behavior. Perhaps the risks involved were themselves the attraction? He built and inaugurated the club in 1971. It has since been counted among the two or three most popular establishments of its kind in the city. The fact that cocaine and other recreational drugs are available on the premises is widely known. Also, discreet, expensive prostitutes are in residence. However, no raids or arrests have ever been made at the club. Anonymous informants within the Houston Police Department state that Turrentine's wealth (in influence and payoffs) has protected the club's management and clientele. Further, in this regard, Turrentine's connection with Colombian drug lords has been established: Isaacs has documentation that in 1977, 1979, 1983, 1987, and 1988, Turrentine visited the Rodríguez Orejuela family compound near Cali. Related to these drug connections is the almost-certain connection with offshore money laundering in the Caribbean and Central and South America. The labyrinthine nature of financial transactions in these matters makes it almost impossible to implicate Turrentine directly. Nevertheless, Isaacs believes the FBI and IRS have proof of both drug smuggling and money laundering but are waiting to indict Turrentine until an adequate cadre of credible witnesses can be recruited.

A final observation by Isaacs has to do with Turrentine's heavy financial investment in Enron. The company has made phenomenal profits and has expanded to become one of the top ten corporations in the United States. Isaacs has information from within the company that accounting practices have been manipulated in such a way as to hide losses to keep stock prices high. A record of Turrentine's trading in the stock would suggest that he is privy to inside information: His profits have been in the neighborhood of half a billion dollars over the period 1992–98.

Isaacs ends his account of Turrentine with the comment that in many ways, he is the "quintessential postmodern capitalist of the latter twentieth century—unlike Bill Gates and Steve Jobs, who belong in a long line of one-company men such as John Davison

Rockefeller, Henry Ford and Cornelius Vanderbilt, people who, no matter how ruthless, have operated largely within the letter of the law. Turrentine, conversely, is a multiple investor, looking for the main chance anywhere in the global economy that seems favorable, whether legal or illegal. He has no loyalty to any one enterprise. There is, however, a pattern of loyalty to employees in his various operations. His considerable philanthropic contributions to organizations such as the Houston Museum and Opera and the Pasadena Children's Hospital, of which he is a board member, may represent an earnest interest in the community, or they may be smoke screen for his criminal activities."

None of Isaacs' revelations surprise me, but it is satisfying to have the facts and suppositions of an expert to back up my hunches. And yet knowledge of Turrentine's legitimate and criminal activities gets us no closer to a solution in the case of Lila's murder. I didn't, and don't, believe he had any connection to her death, nor do I believe he knew anything about Goon, or about Buck's involvement in the drug smuggling enterprise of which Lila seems to have been the brains. As far as I'm concerned, the primary suspect was and still is Goon, with Buck Wallace implicated to some undetermined degree.

Gwen's surprise gourmet supper is *Carbounado* served with a Napa Valley Cabernet Sauvignon. She begins the meal with a French soup, *aïgo boulido,* and ends with a delicious fruit dessert she tells me is *poires et coings au miel.* I haven't eaten so well in a long while. By the time I've finished, I am flushed with love and goodwill.

"Where in the world do you find all the ingredients for this wonderful stuff?" I ask her.

"*In the world!* There are a few specialty shops in Great Falls. Then I rummage the catalogues for what I can't get there or in Helena. Sometimes Lev Geoffroy at the Lewis and Clark Hotel orders special cuts of meat for me. He got me this mutton. . . . So you like my cooking?"

"Like it? Damned right I like it! It kick-starts my appetite for you . . . but let's wait until these initial courses settle a bit before we get to the pièce de résistance."

I haven't told Gwen but Laura had not the foggiest notion how to cook. She was satisfied if I grilled a steak or chicken legs while she boiled some rice and steamed broccoli on the stove. Other times she "fixed" precooked Stouffer's meals in the microwave. She was always too busy with her schoolwork or some feminist activity to think much about food. My grandmother, who raised me from my third year, was an excellent cook, but knew only Old Dominion cuisine: Brunswick stew, baked turkey at Thanksgiving and Christmas, butter beans cooked with bacon or fatback, stewed tomatoes, overcooked snap beans, spoon bread, biscuits, and so forth. Until I met Gwen, all my elegant dining had been confined to restaurants. Several of Laura's and my friends in Chicago cooked gourmet meals—very occasional fare for me. But here was the real thing—in Clark City, Montana!

"Where did you learn to cook like that?" I ask as we clear away the dishes.

"I thought I told you before."

"You did, a little, but I want to hear it again. It does my soul and stomach good."

"Your soul and stomach seem to have a very intimate connection."

"As Walt Whitman said, soul and stomach should walk hand in hand. . . ."

She runs hot water in the sink and hands me a dish towel.

"Okay," she says. "After Charlie and I got married out in Seattle, he was so busy with his graduate work, day and night, I found myself with a lot of time in my lap. I worked as an admin assistant at the engineering school, but there was nothing to do after work but watch television or read. Charlie didn't like my going out to movies by myself, but he didn't mind my taking classes. I started with literature courses, then got interested in cooking and spent four semesters in an adult ed class at night taught by one of the best chefs in Seattle. No college credits, and no certification as a *saucier*, but I got good enough that Sam—the chef—said he'd get me a job in a first-class restaurant if I wanted. Our marriage wasn't working out; Charlie was becoming abusive. Meanwhile, my interest in medicine was growing.

"You know how you are at that age. How you develop unrealistic models based on your heroes. I'd been reading a lot of Chekhov and William Carlos Williams. When Charlie and I split, I started medical school. After a year I decided an M.D. would take too long and transferred to the nursing program. I got my master's degree, came back to Montana, and sat for the nurse-practitioner's exam.

"So here I am, but I never gave up my interest in cooking—I have a book full of notes I took in Sam's classes. The meal I fixed tonight was based on recipes I took down while he was experimenting with Provençal cuisine. I've done that meal three or four times in the past. It's always turned out excellent. . . . End of story."

"Well, see. That's the good thing about retelling stories. You included some things there you never told me before—about you and Charlie particularly. You need to tell me that whole story sometime."

Spook has gotten up from his mat in the corner and gone to the back door. At first he whines a bit. Then he starts to bark.

"He never does that unless there's someone there at the door," Gwen says.

We wait to see if someone will knock. Then I get up, flick on the back stoop light, and open the door. It's very dark in the yard, but I glimpse someone hurrying off into the night. I also realize I'm not wearing the .38 Ralston gave me. What would I have done if someone had been standing there with a gun pointed at me? What would I have done even if I had the .38? Someone was definitely there, probably up on the stoop, listening to our conversation.

"Gwen, do you have a gun besides that 20-gauge Superposed Diana you use for birds?"

"I've got a little Wilkinson .25 I keep in my dresser and sometimes carry around in my purse."

"Well, somebody was out there. Who and for what reason, your guess is as good as mine. It's a good thing I'm spending the night. Show me where you keep the .25."

"You're right. Spook never lies about that. He never barks unless somebody comes up on the stoop or the front porch. He's really good about that."

I'm awake half the night listening for noises outside. Waiting for Spook to bark. I slip off to sleep, then wake with a snap. That's the way I was the first few weeks in Vietnam.

Chapter Twelve

THIS MORNING, AFTER COOKING BREAKFAST AND SEEING GWEN OFF to work, I search the backyard for clues as to who visited us last night. The ground is frozen solid, so no tracks, and there's nothing else but the dead grass, shrubs, trees, and some old paint buckets Gwen hasn't gotten around to taking to the Dempsey Dumpsters. I check the stoop but no clues there either. I guess it could have been Buck Wallace—he's probably getting pretty antsy wondering what I know about the case. I hope he hasn't found out that I talked with Jeremy Toussaint, but he must know by now that I've been deputized. There is also the possibility that Goon has returned, which gives me the chills. Nonetheless I hope he's come back because we're not going to make any progress on the case until he shows his hand. Since there's nothing more I can do at Gwen's, I drive over to my bungalow and call Ralston.

"Any word on Turrentine?"

"Yeah, Jake. His office called yesterday. Said he was in Argentina seeing to business. He plans to return to the U.S. next week. I asked them to have him call me. Not much else I can do on the case until then. . . . I'm still trying to chase down those bank robbers, a Bonnie and Clyde pair. Their car was spotted by some town cop in Nebraska the day before yesterday, but they gave him the slip and nobody has seen hide nor hair of them since. This guy you call Goon is still a mystery. Both the Butte and Great Falls police are trying to get an ID on the prints in the two cars. They match each other, but nobody can find a match in any of the state or national files. The FBI is checking for us with Interpol. Hope they turn up something."

He asks how it's going on my end, and I tell him about the visitor to Gwen's place last night.

"Watch out, Jake. I'm sure that big guy is dangerous. . . . Dimitri! What a hell of a name. Let me know immediately if you get a bead on him."

I want to call Jeremy to ask if he's seen Goon or learned anything from Wallace, but I'm afraid Buck will answer the phone. I could always hang up, but he'd probably guess it was me or someone else trying to get in touch with Jeremy. I decide to wait for Jeremy to call me. At least that will give me a chance to work on the novel.

Just after four o'clock, Carlton calls and says he needs to come over and talk to me.

"Sure, Carlton. It's about toddy time anyway."

I already have a Black Jack and water poured when he arrives.

He tells me he went out to the Circle 9 this morning, pretending to do some finish work on the barn. Buck came outside as soon as he pulled up in the driveway.

"I could tell he was real nervous. Wanted to know what I was doing out there. I told him I had a little more work to do on the loft. Wouldn't take more than a couple of hours. He acted like I was an unwashed aborigine, but he told me to go ahead. I fiddled around in the barn for a while. When I saw Jeremy walk across the yard toward the guesthouse, I went back to my truck like I was fetching more tools. He sees me and comes out in the yard. 'How are you, Mr. Heavy-Eagle?' He likes to call me that. I tell him I'm fine and ask how he and Olivia are doing. 'We're passing well,' he says, but then he lowers his voice and tells me that big ugly man Bat was out there yesterday. 'I'm afraid to call Mr. Battle,' he said. 'Mr. Turrentine has the phones fixed so you can listen in from his office—even the guesthouse phone. I think Mr. Buck has turned on the recording machine in there.'

"Jeremy also told me that Bat arrived in his plane and Buck met him out at the strip, then they went into the house and talked for a while. Last night Bat drove off in the station wagon and returned after midnight. This morning he got in his plane and left just after daylight. Jeremy tried to get the numbers off the wing and tail, but it was too far to see, even with Mrs. Turrentine's binoculars. 'You tell Mr. Battle. I'm afraid of that man Bat,' and it seemed he wanted to tell me more but about that time Buck came back out of the house and walked over to the truck, so we pretended to be talking about who would be making the NFL playoffs. Jeremy goes on about how 'there ain't nothing to do out there anymore since Mrs. Turrentine passed but watch television. I'm sure glad Mr. Turrentine got that big dish antenna year before last,' he says, like that's all we have been talking about. 'Mr. Heavy-Eagle thinks the Seahawks are going to win the Super Bowl this year. They might just do that.' Jeremy tells me to come on up to the house and ask Olivia if I need anything to eat or drink, then he goes back in the house."

Buck had waited for Jeremy to leave and then asked if Carlton was finished with the barn.

"He said he didn't want me coming back out there. Not until Mr. Turrentine gets back and says whether he wants me to work on the barn anymore. 'That was Mrs. Turrentine's idea, not his. You stay away until I tell you it's all right to come back.' So I got my tools from the barn and came back to town.

"That big guy can fly in and out as he likes and we won't know anything about it. I bet he don't even file a flight plan."

I tell Carlton about somebody being in Gwen's backyard last night, and what the Butte police found out about Goon.

"Dimitri! He must be some Ruskie son of a wench. I bet he's up to something, Jake. Bet he's going to cause some real trouble soon. I'm keeping my .38 with me all the time now. I keep the .270 on the rack with me in the truck too."

After Carlton leaves, I try to work on the novel, but about seven, Gwen calls.

"Jake, can you come over here right now? I've got a message on the answering machine you need to listen to."

Her voice has a sharp edge on it. When I get there and she opens the door, I can tell she's really upset.

"Christ, Jake. I think it must be that big guy. The one you call Goon . . . Dimitri, or whatever his name is. I'll bet he was the one in the backyard last night."

I tell her what Jeremy told Carlton this afternoon. Then she plays the message. The voice sounds rough, like the guy has a hard time talking, like something is wrong with his larynx. He also has a strong accent, but I can't place it. I'd guess somewhere in Central or Eastern Europe.

"Miss Yefferson. I friend Lila Turrentine. . . . She wast wan ugly beetch. Real ugly. She meant to die. I see you last night. Your ugly boyfriend too. You tell Battle I see hem. Tell hem I don't like his face. Tell him he real ugly. You too. Real ugly. I going to make sure you don't make no ugly chil'ren. You tell hem. Tell hem leave me alone. I get hem good. I fix his ugly face."

As he goes on the voice gets angrier and angrier, then breaks into a language I don't recognize, but it sounds more Arabic than Slavic. Then he speaks in broken English again.

"I break Jake Battle neck. I do things you before I break your neck. Tell Indian I get hem too. He real ugly. All you ugly people, you die. You die like Lila. Soon I get you all."

There is a pause, then the click as he hangs up. It can't be anybody but Goon. But where did he call from? Is he back out at the Circle 9, or did he call long distance from wherever he flew to this morning? And what's his beef with us? Buck must have told him I've been deputized to investigate the murder, and that Gwen and Carlton are my friends.

Gwen has been pacing the room as the message played. She stops in front of me.

"Jesus, Jake, I'm scared. You reckon that was that Dimitri? I guess it couldn't be anyone else. We've got to do something."

"I don't know what we can do right now. I can't drive out to the Circle 9 every couple of hours just to see if he's come back. But you're staying over at my place from now on. Until this Goon is in jail or dead."

"What do you think all this 'ugly' business is about? He's one of the ugliest men I've ever seen, and here he is calling us all ugly, like that was the number one word in his vocabulary."

"I don't know . . . but get your things together. You may have to stay over at my place for quite a while."

As we drive to my bungalow, Spook stands on the back seat, facing forward so his head is between ours. He looks expectantly out into the night, like he knows something's up and is ready to do something about it. He is one of the smartest dogs I've ever known. Gwen has him trained to do most anything she wants. But it isn't just training; it's intelligence, as if he figures things out on his own and does them to please her. She can say, "Spook, get my slippers," and he'll go to the bedroom and get her slippers. She has duck decoys all over her apartment. She'll say, "Spook, go get the blue-winged teal," and Spook will get the blue-winged teal, or the mallard, or the harlequin, or the merganser—whichever one she says.

When we get to my apartment, I call Ralston.

"At least you didn't wait until midnight this time," he says when he picks up the phone. "What is it?"

I tell him about Goon's phone call.

"Sounds like he might be insane, Jake. That makes it even more scary. You want me to send Barney out there in case there's trouble? He could stay at the Bunkhouse."

"What good could Barney do? We'll handle things here until something definite breaks. You think I could tell Tim Free what's going on and get him to help? I know he talks a lot, but he can keep quiet if he needs to."

"I guess so, Jake. He'd be more help than Barney if it came to a shoot-out."

He tells me to make a copy of the phone call on my tape recorder: "Maybe somebody at the FBI can analyze it—at least find out what language the guy was speaking."

I tell him okay, then call the Bunkhouse to see if Carlton's in. Bunny answers the phone.

"Not here, Jake. He went over to the Antler about an hour ago. . . . How are you doing? Any breaks on the murder?"

I tell her we're following up on a couple of leads, but nothing is certain, so I can't say who the suspects might be.

"I'll bet that creep Buck Wallace is one of them. I've never liked that son of a gun. Bob says he makes his flesh crawl whenever he sees him. . . . Good luck on getting the scoundrel."

I call the Antler and get Nerice to hand the phone to Carlton. I tell him about Gwen's call from Goon and the threats he made.

"I'll watch out, Jake. I'm going to drink just a couple tonight."

"Remember you had two over here at my place. You stay sober."

"You betcha, Jake. I'll be careful. You and Gwen be careful too."

I ask him if Tim Free is around. He isn't, so I call Jody's. When he takes the phone, I ask if he can come over to my bungalow for a few minutes.

His first words when he walks in the door are: "What's up, Jake. You want to borrow my hat?"

When I tell him what we've learned about the murder and ask if he's willing to help if things start popping, he drops the comedy routine.

"You betcha, Jake. You got my telephone number and you know where I hang out. I keep my .308 in the truck. My .357 Magnum too. I'll be on the lookout for this Dimitri. I think I saw him once, riding around with Buck Wallace in Turrentine's Yukon. And, yeah, I'll stay quiet about all this. I know you don't want to let Buck think you know about him. I'll be ready whenever you need me."

Before Gwen and I go to bed, I make sure Spook is strategically stationed near the back door.

Chapter Thirteen

YESTERDAY GWEN HAD TO OPEN THE CLINIC FOR HALF A DAY, SO I TOOK my PowerBook over and set up in one of the examining rooms. Seemed half the county came in for flu shots, or they already had the flu and came in to be treated. The state lets her keep a variety of medicines at the clinic and dispense them at bargain rates since it's so far to the nearest drug stores in Great Falls and Helena. It was after seven o'clock when she finally locked the door.

"Let's go over to Jody's and get a pizza, Jake. I'm too bushed to cook."

Tim Free was at the bar telling his jokes. It's amazing how many of them are new. I don't know where he gets them. Maybe he makes them up. When he saw us, he came over to the table with news about Buck Wallace.

"He was at the Antler all afternoon, Jake. He nursed a couple of beers and pretended to be watching the game on TV, but he was listening to every conversation in the room. I watched him the whole time out of the corner of my eye. I guess he's pretty nervous. I asked him how things were out at the Circle 9. Told him a couple of jokes. He didn't laugh, just gave me a nervous grin. That son of a bitch needs to have his asshole irrigated. He left about an hour ago. He was in the GMC pickup. He usually don't drive that."

This morning Gwen cooks a big Sunday breakfast of herring and grits with lots of coffee. We read newspaper articles to each other as we eat. More Y2K doom. It's getting close now—less than two weeks. There's also more Monica Lewinski rubbish, which sends Gwen into a rant that I know better than to interrupt.

"What the hell does anyone care if Willie Jeff Clinton got his whistle blown in the Oval Office! Consensual sex! Let him get all he needs. Calms him down to run the country and not get us involved in those damned Republican pseudo wars. That's what Nixon and Reagan and Bush needed—blow jobs in the White House. Would have improved their dispositions and kept us out of trouble. . . . I wish Clinton had just 'fessed up, though. That would have taken the wind out of their sails. . . ."

Gwen is a true liberal in a land of rabid conservatives. Most Montanans just hate big government—any kind of federal involvement. It's understandable. In a way they are truly democratic: They believe in absolute equality—among Caucasians, that is. Native Americans and ethnic minorities are another matter. Montanan values are traditional American ones: self-reliance, the right to bear arms, laissez faire politics and business, and so forth. But because of their bucolic naïveté, they don't understand the problems created by racial, capitalistic, and urban oppression. The very idea of social welfare goes against their beliefs in individual autonomy. Gwen and her family are an anomaly in the little town of Wolf Creek. Their neighbors still have Reagan and Bush stickers plastered all over their pickups, and some still have Dole signs stuck in their lawns. I listen to her rage on: "That oily little prick Ken Starr. The whole investigation makes me sick. And now Monica thinks she's big stuff and is going to clean up on the publicity ... make herself a fortune. Jesus Christ!" She loves Montana but abhors its politics, and doesn't hesitate to speak her mind.

A couple of months ago we were having a drink at Jody's and talking about the prospect of fishing the South Fork of the Flathead next summer. At the next table, a bunch of ranchers and outfitters were railing vociferously at Clinton and Gore, and particularly at Hillary. They were lamenting welfare, environmental protection, the possibility of socialized medicine—everything Gwen and I support. I could see she was getting steamed. Finally, she couldn't ignore them anymore and said in a loud voice, "What a bunch of sap-headed know-nothings you obsolescent cowboys are. Bill Clinton is twice as smart as any damned Republican who's been in Washington since Teddy Roosevelt. He's trying to do what's best for the country despite all you self-righteous plutocrats and your political lackeys."

Gwen has a tongue. Even though I agreed with everything she said, I was embarrassed—not for her but for the recipients of her harangue. And she was just getting warmed up: "Look at Nixon! A clever, slimy petty criminal, but not nearly clever enough. Look at Reagan—dumbest nerd ever to inhabit the White House. If you'd given him a globe and asked him to point to Iran, he'd have gotten lost in the steppes of Mongolia, or the ice sheets of Antarctica. All the moms and pops loved him because he talked to them on television in that treacly Hollywood voice, smiling his big studio smile. What a bloody, empty-headed fraud he was!"

The men shifted around in their seats and looked uneasily at one another. Because of their ingrained gallantry, Gwen had an unfair advantage. They didn't try to rebut her. Instead they talked quietly about beef prices and the weather. But Gwen was still steaming: "Hey, Jody, bring me another drink—a double scotch on the rocks. And have you got any air freshener? There's a decide moral stench over here in our area."

When her drink came, she stared them all down as she sipped. Slowly they got up one by one and sauntered lamely over to the bar to pay their bills. When the last one had gone, Gwen looked at me sheepishly.

"I'm sorry, Jake. I just can't abide their stupidity. They're all nice people—wonderful wives. But they're stupid, just stupid. What can you do with stupidity?"

"I don't know, darling. But you were magnificent. The DNC should give you an honorary title—Gwenie, the Pachyderm Killer. They should hire you for the debates. I didn't think those self-righteous wranglers could be routed. But by God, you did it. Here, let me buy you a steak."

After we've cleaned the dishes and made the bed, Gwen remembers that she has reports to fill out at the clinic. I walk over with her and read through a half-dozen magazines in the waiting room while she fills out the forms and puts them in envelopes to mail tomorrow.

"Jake, I love this job," she says when she comes out of her office. "I like helping people, particularly people who really need help, but damned the bureaucracies. It seems I spend a third of my time going to meetings in Helena and filling out reports. That doesn't leave much time when I'm not with patients to read the journals and keep up with all the new research and treatment. Sometimes I get up early and read for a couple of hours before opening the clinic. When am I ever going to get back to Chekhov and Tolstoy? What's that the old woman servant—Agatha Mikhailovna—in *Anna Karenina* says? 'The first thing you've got to think about is your soul'? Let's go back to your place and read a book."

The temperature is five above today. But we've had no significant snow for a couple of weeks. On the walk home, I notice isolated patches of snow on the lawns that give the grass a brindled look. There is no wind, so the sun delivers a modicum of warmth. But high over the white-cloaked Front Range, a veil of cirrus clouds moves eastward. We'll have more snow before the week is out. Let it come. We need the snowpack in the mountains.

In Nam, I could never stop sweating. The sun beat down like a sledgehammer. The night was a hyper-saturated sauna. I'd wake with water trickling from my pores, burning my eyes, my bedding soaked like a washrag. And the mosquitoes always took their pint of blood.

The bite of zero degrees is small price for immunity from mosquitoes and that searing heat.

The only times I was cold in 'Nam were the days after Sonny Gupton tripped a land mine. We'd been separated from the platoon, and the two of us were making our way to our rendezvous point before the Hueys whirled in to shuttle us back to base. I knew the area was heavily mined and kept reminding Gupton to watch for trip wires and triggers. He was a scrawny, dull-eyed kid from eastern North Carolina, who always seemed half-unconscious except during our baseball and volleyball games. Sure enough, he stumbled over a trip wire. I was lucky the mine was on the other side of him. Most of the metal caught him waist high. His torso was almost completely separated from his lower body; even his backbone was torn in half. Dead . . . dead before his forehead hit the ground. His life was my aegis. Quite so, but one big piece of hot shrapnel got around or through him, and ripped into my right thigh just below the buttock. I knew I was hit but at first couldn't tell where. I lay on the ground I don't know how long trying to decide if I was going to die. At first I was sure I would—in the sweltering, outlandish jungle nine thousand miles from home. A part of me wished I'd ease out of this world and find peace and rest somewhere beyond, as I'd wished several times lately a Cong bullet would find my brain cleanly through the center of my forehead. So I just lay there waiting for the denouement. All was still and the sky was a heavenly blue. Eventually I ran my hands over my upper body several times before I went lower and found the wound. I decided I might survive. Slowly the desire to live returned, and I lay there in a kind of euphoria, feeling the bugs crawl across my arms, down my neck, into my boots. At least I could feel. A blue beauty came out of the weeds near my feet and slithered along, passing eight inches from my head. When his tail disappeared into a clump of grass, I crawled over to check Gupton for a sign of pulse, knowing that there would be none. Then I cut away my pant leg with my survival knife and fixed a compress over the wound. For an hour I hobbled to the rendezvous point, using my M-16 as a cane. Fortunately one of the Hueys had come back to look for Gupton and me. I had lost a lot of blood. I felt like I was freezing. When they loaded me aboard, I asked for blankets—I kept asking for blankets while the medics pumped me back up with plasma. I didn't feel warm again until my second or third day in the hospital at Kishine Barracks.

Maybe cold weather should be my *memento mori.* Probably it is. But the oppressive Vietnam jungles are still strong in my memory. This frigid Montana air is my relief and deliverance.

Chapter Fourteen

MONDAY MORNING RALSTON CALLS TO TELL ME THAT TURRENTINE WILL fly into Helena on Tuesday. Ralston had talked him into landing there instead of the ranch to give us a chance to talk to him without Buck knowing. Turrentine would stay in Helena for only one night, though, because he needed to be in Houston from the twenty-third until after Christmas.

"Something to do with contingency plans in case Y2K turns out to be as bad as some experts predict," Ralston says. "What do you think, Jake? You believe all our computers are going to go haywire?"

"I hope not, but I've made copies of all my work files and financial statements just in case. I think the computer whizzes have probably worked out most of the kinks. I'm sure we'll sail right on into the new millennium on a strong tailwind."

"Well, I hope so, Jake"

He tells me they caught the Bonnie and Clyde pair.

"Dumb klutzes tried to rob a bank in Dubuque. Driving the same car, same license. The Iowa state patrol had them in a ditch before they got ten miles out of town. They had nearly all the money from Montana First in the trunk. No shoot-out, though. They gave up without a shot."

"I hope this Lila case ends as peaceably, but I doubt it will."

I ask him what time I should be at the station Tuesday.

"We're meeting at the Bar None out on Cedar Street at three o'clock. Turrentine and I both thought it best if he wasn't seen downtown."

I buy Ralston a beer while we wait for Turrentine.

"You seem pretty sure that Turrentine wasn't involved in the murder—or the cocaine running, Jake. Can you rule him out?"

"I can't rule anything out for sure, but the drug business seems to have been entirely Lila's concern—a way to support her habit and make a little mad money on the side. She wouldn't have wanted Randal to know anything about it. That's why he exiled her up here in the first place—to get her away from the drug scene in Houston."

I confess to sandbagging and tell him about Isaacs' summary of Turrentine's legal and illegal enterprises.

"I got it from some guy down at Rice University—a friend of a friend. Everything points to Turrentine being involved in big-time drug running. Lila's piddling shipments would seem like chicken scratch to Randal. Appears he's into money laundering too."

I tell him about Jon Erickson having gotten wind of an FBI investigation.

"Why haven't I got wind of it? I'm the sheriff. Why didn't the FBI let me know they're after him? You seem to always be a couple of furlongs ahead of me, Jake. What the hell else do you know?"

"Not much, really. Just more details about his business dealings. Those things don't really concern us. They don't have anything to do with Lila's murder. We're trying to get that solved, and in that endeavor Turrentine is on our side. Let's just go through what questions we want to ask him. Let's pretend he's a law-abiding citizen."

"Well, Jake, since you have a better handle on this case than I do, I'm going to let you ask the questions and do the talking. I'll just butt in if I see something you're missing."

At three-thirty Randal shows up with his bodyguard, apologizes for being late, and orders a martini. He tells Modell to wait for him in the bar.

"So you think Buck is involved in Lila's murder, Mr. Battle . . . Jake," he says as soon as Modell is out of earshot. "Can you be sure? He's always been a loyal and honest operative for me."

I repeat what Jeremy told me about Lila and Goon and Buck.

Turrentine's response is that Buck probably got involved against his better judgment: "Lila probably coerced him into cooperating. . . . Do you think he was sleeping with her?"

"I have no idea . . . but I think he stole Carlton Heavy-Eagle's rifle. I think Buck was jealous or angry because he found out Carlton was sleeping with Lila and was intending to get revenge somehow. But I'm pretty sure he wasn't at Golden Meadows when she was killed. I don't think he knew the big guy was going to kill her."

Turrentine finishes his drink and signals the bartender to bring another.

"I just can't believe Lila would have been stupid enough to get into cocaine trafficking. . . . You guessed why I kept her up here, didn't you? I thought you would. . . . Should I confront Buck? I think he'd tell me the truth."

"If you did that, Randal, I don't think we'd ever get the big guy, Dimitri. Dimitri Ivanovich Sulamanov—that's the handle he's going under."

"Who is this guy?"

I tell him what we know about Goon, which isn't much.

"Did Lila own a .32 pistol?" I ask.

"Yes, a little Walther PPK I bought for her ten or eleven years ago. I haven't seen it since last summer. Why do you ask?"

I explain that somebody shot twice with a .32 out at Golden Meadows, and that we think maybe Lila was defending herself when Dimitri tried to shoot her.

"Well, I hope she hit the SOB if she did. She was an excellent shot. I taught her myself."

I ask him more questions about Buck and Jeremy and Olivia but don't find out anymore than I already know. I watch him closely throughout our conversation. He seems to be candid in his answers and comments. He's a smooth operator. I guess he has to be, the way he runs his businesses. So I spring Lila's porn photos on him. He doesn't blink.

"Damn. Are those pictures still around? I paid the guy who took them a hunk of money to destroy them. A professional glamor photographer named Karl Mueller. I didn't know about the photos until we'd been married four or five years. One of my colleagues saw them on the Web—Mueller evidently has his own porn site. I asked Lila about them. She said she'd done them for kicks shortly after she moved to New York. She had tendencies—I found out about that later. As far as she knew, they had never been published in the men's magazine Mueller worked for, so she thought they were stored away safely in his files. I got in touch with Mueller, told him who I was, and asked if he could get them off the Web. I offered him money, but he said he'd do it gratis, would never have put them up if he'd known Lila had married me. I sent him ten grand anyway—to keep him honest. He warned me that once pictures were put on the Web, anyone could download them, and they might show up again on an unauthorized site. I guess that's what happened. No need to worry about them anymore—Lila is beyond defamation now. . . . How did the photos look—I've never seen them."

"They're real professional work," I tell him. "She's beautiful. They're good . . . real good."

At ten of five Randal asks if we have all the information we need from him.

"I've got to be off for Seattle, then New York, then Houston. We have to make sure all the accounts are covered with backup zip disks in case our hard drives get erased. My programmers tell me everything is covered, but you never know. . . . Can one of you give us a ride back to the airport? We had to take a taxi over here."

We collect Modell from the bar and I take the two of them out to Excel Aviation, where Turrentine's Learjet is being serviced.

"You want to see inside, Jake? It's a custom job."

I go aboard for the tour. It is a beauty. Rich cream leather upholstery throughout. Four deep lounge seats that can be made into sleeping couches. A bar. A big sleeping couch at the rear with folding panels to close it off from the rest of the plane. A watertight toilet compartment that also has a shower nozzle. A sink just outside. A galley with refrigerator underneath. A shielded microwave. A fold-down desk with computer connections. A 36-inch flat-screen TV with VCR and DVD player. A CD sound system. A conference table that swings down from the bulkhead. It's like something out of a James Bond movie. Scott Dawkins, Randal's personal pilot, is a slim, handsome guy, six-foot-two, forty-five years old or so. He shows me around the cockpit, telling me about the various instruments and the advanced GPS navigation system. The Wulfsberg Flight Phone. The Collins Radar Altimeter.

"A sixty model, Jake. I've had it six years. Scott babies it. The folks at Bombardier say it will fly forever. . . . I'm the copilot, Jake—Not God, mind you. But I'm pretty good—top instrument rating. Landed once in Newfoundland in a fog you could have swum in."

Scott nods his head in affirmation and smiles. I shake hands with all three men, wish them a pleasant flight and depart, wondering what all the plane has witnessed. Orgies? Criminal collusion? Murders? The signing of contracts worth millions . . . billions? Transport of celebrities? Hollywood goddesses? Big-time CEOs? Warlords? Racketeering kingpins? Drug moguls? My head is spinning with possibilities as I wheel along the interstate headed north. The cloud cover is lowering. I expect snow will start falling before I get back home.

The snow has been coming down for two days. Not a blizzard—there's not much wind, but big flakes are falling so thickly at times you can see scarcely a hundred yards. In the morning I go over to the clinic with Gwen, but only four patients show up, so we lock up at three o'clock and head to Jody's for a late lunch. Both Tim Free and Carlton are there drinking beer. Tim comes over before we sit down and kneels in front of Gwen, looking intently at her knees.

"What the hell are you doing, you squirt?"

"Checking to see if you're getting any more bowlegged. Doesn't look like she is, Jake. You need a wider-brimmed hat."

Gwen asks Tim if he soaks his brain in a toilet every night.

Carleton comes over: "Buck Wallace came to town this morning, Jake. In the GMC pickup. Jeremy was with him. They went into Tomaski's to get supplies. Then they stopped at Janie's. Buck went in and left Jeremy in the truck with the motor running. I was watching from the lobby at the Bunkhouse, so I walked over and asked Jeremy if Buck was inside eating. 'Yes, he is, Mr. Heavy-Eagle. Said he was getting himself a cheeseburger. He's bringing me a hamburger and fries. . . . Said the white folks up here didn't like niggers and wouldn't want me in their restaurant.' 'I never heard such shit, Jeremy.' I tell him I'll take him inside, but he says he better not go in. He knows folks don't mind because Miss Lila took him in there several times. Into the Antler bar too, but he doesn't want to get Mr. Buck upset. Jeremy also tells Carlton that Bat hasn't been back to the ranch since last Friday.

" 'Mr. Buck's been on the phone to him several times, though. I try to listen, but I haven't heard much. I did hear him say that Mr. Turrentine is coming back Wednesday of next week. Several times I heard him say, "Stay away, stay away." He said it pretty loud, like he was scared.'

"I told Jeremy he shouldn't be sitting in a pickup with the motor running in weather like this—he might die of carbon monoxide poisoning—and invited him to wait in the Bunkhouse, but he said he'd be all right, that he was keeping the window cracked."

Gwen and I order buffalo burgers, which are better than the beef burgers. The meat is fresher and doesn't have all the fat. Johnson Clyde runs two hundred head out on the Bar Ten. Lonnie Demarest, who works for Albertson's, comes out from Helena every couple of months and does the butchering, and Jody buys directly from Johnson. I think they forego the FDA inspections. Anyway, it's excellent meat, and you can eat it rare without fear of E. coli.

We decide to stay awhile. A lot of townsfolk are coming in to celebrate Christmas Eve. About nine-thirty there is a great influx, services at the several churches having concluded. The atmosphere is festive. Last week Jody decorated the place with strings of lights, little light-filled Santa Clauses and Rudolphs here and there, pine garlands, and a Christmas tree. She's also loaded the sound system with Christmas CDs—Kathleen Battle, Mel Tormé, Robert Shaw, Thomas Hampson. But no Lawrence Welk or Perry Como or muzak—she has taste. Everybody is convivial and merry. That's one of the things I like about Clark City: its communal spirit is natural and generous, unlike the neurotic chumminess of so many big city pubs and bars.

At ten o'clock, Tim Free parades out of the pantry dressed in a Santa Claus outfit. After making the rounds of the room to wish everyone a Merry Christmas, he sits in a big chair, center-floor, with his back to the pool table, and invites all the women to sit in his lap and tell him what they want stuffed into their pantyhose tonight. They whisper in his ear, he whispers in theirs, and they both have a good laugh. Later, Gus Fox takes center stage and recites "The Night Before Christmas" entirely from memory, adding an epilogue that Clement Moore could never have written. Then we all sing carols to Louise Duncan's accompaniment on the upright piano: "God Rest You, Merry Gentlemen," "It Came Upon the Midnight Clear," "Hark! the Herald Angels Sing," "O Little Town of Bethlehem," "Silent Night." By eleven everyone is rosy, and the Christmas spirit has even moved Jody to serve drinks on the house. But Gwen and I are bushed, so we wish all a good night and trudge to my house through the snow, which is a foot and a half deep on the lawns and rooftops and four inches on the scraped streets. I wrap my arm around Gwen:

"I wonder if something important did happen on a midnight

clear about two-thousand years ago. It seems a lot of people believe it did. Was it Yeats' 'uncontrollable mystery'? Or was it something else? Or *nada*?"

"I don't know, Jake. If only all this Jesus stuff were true! God-damn it, it breaks my heart when I think of all these Christians wanting peace and goodwill. The world is so fucked up, and they're trying to tell us that God has a plan and all the starving kids and wars and earthquakes and floods are a part of his design and that everything will come out all right in the end. How can they believe it? I wish I could believe it. Every time a kid dies, I wonder what kind of god could be in charge? Yet I don't doubt that they want peace and love and goodness to reign. It's the damned difference between what they pray for and what *is* that breaks my heart. Our spirits yearn for the ideal, but our behavior just perpetuates the everlasting moral chaos."

She starts to cry a little, so I hold her tight and let her sob. The snow is coming down gentler now. It makes a hushed brushing noise as it caresses our clothes. There's a break in the cloud cover, and for a few moments the moon shines through. It is just past full. In the soft luminous glow I can see out across the hills an unbroken blanket of whiteness attempting to cover over the multitudinous blemishes of the world.

Chapter Fifteen

THIS MORNING I GET UP EARLY SO GWEN CAN SLEEP IN WHILE I FIX breakfast. Before going to the kitchen, I get the Winston rod out of the closet and put it under our tree. A few days ago, when the back roads were still passable, I drove out to my property in Finnegan's Gulch, ostensibly to turn the logs for my cabin but really to cut a Christmas tree. In Surry County where I grew up, my grandfather and I went out into the fields every Christmas season to cut down a cedar. When I got old enough to hunt quail, we left the ax at home and on the way back to Grandpa's car with the dogs we'd stop and use our shotguns to shoot a tree off at ground level. That constituted one of my chief pleasures when I was a kid. That and the smell of Christmas morning: the heady cedar aroma; the fragrance of oak logs crackling in the fireplace; the under-scent of raisins, citrus fruit, and nuts in my stocking; the mouthwatering bouquets of turkey, wheat rolls, vegetables, and pudding cooking in the kitchen. Those are moments one would like to prolong forever.

Out at my ranch, as I like to call it, there are lots of cedars on the hills. I found one seven feet tall with a pleasingly full but attenuated shape. The same day I brought it home, Gwen and I decorated the tree with lights and ornaments I bought at Larry's Hardware. It looks homey standing between the front windows in the living room. It's still too dark to see outside, so I flick on the side-yard spot. I heard the wind picking up during the night, but I'm not prepared for a blizzard: Wind is whipping the snow around in swirls and banners, piling it against trees, heaping it in windrows, covering over shrubs. My yard is a gallery of fanciful shapes: polar bears and swans and unicorns. The street is covered in drifts. We won't be driving to Wolf Creek for dinner with Gwen's family as planned. She'll be disappointed, but maybe the Winston rod and the two bottles of Mumms I'm chilling in the refrigerator will console her. At eight I arrange two cups of coffee, two croissants with shaved butter, and a condiment dish of marmalade on a tray and carry it into the bedroom.

"Wake up, sleepy. I've got the first course of breakfast here for you. Merry Christmas."

She turns over slowly and looks at me quizzically before she smiles.

"Well, if I'm Sleepy, you must be Dopey."

"I'll settle for that, but it looks like we won't be going to commune with the Jeffersons in Wolf Creek this morning."

"What do you mean?"

I pull the curtain back for her to see.

"My God, it's still snowing. A real blizzard. I'll call Mom in a little while. I'll bet the snow is ten feet deep in those big dips out on 287."

She nibbles at her croissant and takes a sip of coffee. A big smile spreads across her face as she looks at me.

"Well, darling, we'll just have to make the best of it in our warm little cottage all by ourselves. We can go over to Wolf Creek when the storm clears next week," she says, her gray-green eyes twinkling.

Her hair is tangled, but there is high color in her cheeks. She never wears makeup—doesn't have to. She looks very fetching sitting up in bed in her flannel pajamas.

"I meant to get up during the night and put your present under the tree . . . but I forgot. I mean I didn't wake up. It's under the bed. You can have it now if you want."

"After breakfast," I say.

While she finishes the croissant, I go back to the kitchen and finish cooking. A simple repast: eggs over light, bacon, browned challah slices, and grits. When we've finished eating, I break out the champagne, rub the glass rims with a twist of lemon peel, fill the flutes, and propose a toast: "To our first Christmas together. May we have many more. With both of us as happy as I am now."

"You didn't buy me a ring, did you? You better not."

"No. Something better."

I get the rod and hand it to her. She hefts it, then strips away the paper.

"My God, a Winston. How could you afford. . . . Oh, I keep forgetting how rich you are. Like one of the three kings. I guess you just don't seem rich, Jake."

When she takes the rod out of the case and sees that it's a Joan Wulff, she lets out a little scream.

"Christ! I've been wanting one of these ever since I read about them two years ago. How did you know? Now I can hang up that clunky old HMG. I can still use that Battenkill Mark III reel, though. Let's go out and cast in the drifts." She takes a look out the window. "I guess not, the wind is still awfully strong. . . . Oh, I'm forgetting you—*your* present."

She goes in the bedroom and comes back with a box, not wrapped, and hands it to me. I open the box, and inside is another box. I open it. Another box. Six boxes before I finally get down to a wrapped present, which is obviously a book. I peel the paper away: a first printing with the creepy cougar dust jacket of Edward Abbey's *Desert Solitaire,* signed! Good lord, I think, where did she find it? I grab her and hug her. I guess we're both very happy with our presents. We stand like that for several minutes, not talking, just holding each other. Then Gwen leans back and looks at me gravely.

"Jake, what are we going to eat for dinner? Have you got anything we can cook? I'm going to miss that big turkey Mom always bakes . . . and the dressing. We're going to need a proper Christmas dinner."

"I've got one of those small snow geese you gave me in October. It's in the freezer, but we can thaw it in the microwave. It weighs only about four pounds. I've got some wild rice. There must be some vegetables in the refrigerator. . . ."

We manage to scrounge up ingredients for a feast. Then Gwen goes to work, giving me orders about preparing the rice, slicing vegetables, getting together the makings for one of her elegant sauces. She thaws the goose slowly in the microwave, turning it every five minutes. In an hour she has the goose in the oven and the rice and the vegetables prepped. She hunts through the cupboards and finds a can of sliced apples. In another half hour she has a pastry crust made. Ten minutes later she slides an apple pie into the oven.

There's nothing to do now but wait for all to cook. We've finished the first bottle of champagne, so I open the other. While we sip, Gwen calls her mother to tell her we can't make the trip today. They talk for a while. Then she talks with her father. Then her grandmother. Then her aunt. Then her brother and his wife. Then I have to talk to her grandmother and mother and father. He tells me he's just gotten in from feeding the cattle—on snowshoes. Everybody is jolly despite the blizzard. After our long-distance familial communion, Gwen and I go in the living room and sit on pillows in front of the Jøtul stove, watching the flames gutter and flicker.

After a little while, Gwen says, "Jake, I don't want to pry. But we're almost family now. There are a couple of things I've wanted to ask you. You've talked a lot about your grandparents, but I've never heard you say a word about your mother and father. What happened to them? I know from what you've told me that you were raised by your grandmother and grandfather."

"I'm not hiding anything. I don't know why I've never spoken about my father. I guess it's because I don't remember him. He died in 1947, when I was one year old. He was a Marine major in the war. In 1944 his battalion was assigned to defend a small island in the Marianas. It was thought to have some strategic importance—I know this because my grandfather told me the story when I was sixteen years old. The island was attacked by a large Japanese force a couple of weeks after my father's battalion landed. They were greatly outnumbered and didn't have a chance, but they held the Japanese off for three weeks, radioing every day for reinforcements and supplies that never came. They asked for air support, which never came. They asked for naval gun support, which never came. They ran out of ammunition. They ran out of food. Finally, a large number of the Marines tried to get off the island in three LCMs and an OMB that the Navy had left for them. The Japanese blew them out of the water with their artillery and patrol boats. Most of the troops who were left surrendered and were taken to another island, where they were executed or died of torture or starvation. Not a single Marine who surrendered survived. My father and nineteen others hid. They ate coconuts if they could open them, but most of the time they were afraid to try because of the noise. They killed and ate the giant coconut crabs when they could find them. They killed and ate snakes—raw. Sometimes they swam in coves at night and collected abalone and sea crabs that often tore their fingers to shreds. Sometimes they ate bugs and worms. My father told my grandfather, when Grandfather could get him to talk about it, that the worst part was hiding in the jungle underbrush and having Japanese soldiers walk by only a few yards away. My father had malaria. Sometimes when the Japanese walked near, he had to tense every muscle in his body to keep from shaking. He lay there with sweat streaming over his body, waiting for a bullet in the head or a bayonet in the back. Most of his friends were found and killed. My father had to live like that for three months. Then the Japanese abandoned the island. A week later a PT boat came to pick up the survivors. There were seven. Out of a whole battalion, only seven survived.

"My father was sent back to the states and given an easy desk assignment in Brooklyn and allowed to take classes at Columbia law school—he'd completed two years before he volunteered in 1941. The Marines figured school would be better therapy than they could provide in Navy hospitals. He got his law degree in 1946, and the next year he came back to Surry and joined the practice of one of Grandfather's friends. He did well as a lawyer, but Grandfather said you could tell that the horrors he'd endured on the island wouldn't let him rest. When I was born, Grandfather thought the gift of a son might lift him out of his depression, but it didn't. In October 1948—it was a Monday morning—he ate a big breakfast my mother cooked, then walked out to the car to leave for work. When my mother noticed at ten o'clock that the car was still in the driveway, she went out to see what was wrong. My father was sitting behind the wheel, staring straight ahead as if he were starting off on a long journey. He had had a heart attack. Twenty-nine years old and he died of a heart attack.

"My mother never recovered from the shock. She had no job, and no money except for my father's life insurance, so Grandfather and Grandmother took us in. They lived on an old plantation on the banks of the James River, not far from Surry Courthouse. Lower Sheldon Plantation it was called. The house had been built in 1695. It wasn't a big house, but there was plenty of room for the four of us. The plantation itself was over a thousand acres. From the farming and Grandfather's business investments, we had plenty of money and lived comfortably in a modest Old Dominion style. But my mother evidently couldn't endure her life any longer. She'd suffered through the war, expecting an "I regret to inform you . . ." telegram for three long years. Then her husband came home and lived in his own private abyss for three years. And then he died. In December 1949 she drove off a bridge at Bacon's Creek and drowned in twelve feet of water. I suppose she drove off on purpose, but she could have gone to sleep at the wheel. Or she could have had a heart attack herself. No autopsy was performed.

"I don't remember her either. Sometimes I get flashes of her, but I think they're generated by photographs I've seen. I used to go through her photo albums for hours when I was a kid. . . ."

Gwen has been silent, listening to my story. Now she says, "Christ, I'm sorry, Jake. I didn't mean to make you wade into all that sadness. On Christmas too. I'm sorry."

She gives me a kiss and refills my champagne glass. I sip it while she gets up to turn off the wild rice and put the carrots on.

"All that is so distant from me. I can't remember either of them anyway," I tell her when she gets back. "I don't feel any personal loss. It's just a sad story. It makes me sad, but it doesn't make me hurt the way it would had I known them. . . . My grandmother is the one I really miss. She was a gentle and loving woman—she grieved quietly over my father's death the rest of her life. She died while I was in Vietnam. . . . My grandfather was a wonderful father to me, spoiled me but taught me a lot too. He died in 1985 when he was ninety-two years old. I was his sole heir. That's where nine hundred thousand of my great fortune came from. You know the rest."

"Sorry, Jake. Let's rise to a happier note. I love you for all your suffering. It's honest suffering, not some neurotic, late-Romantic, twentieth-century angst. I want to make you happy. I promise I'll try. . . . Let's go get dinner on the table."

Chapter Sixteen

THE MEAL IS A MIRACULOUS SUCCESS. SOMEWHERE IN MY PANTRY, Gwen discovered a jar of apricot preserves I didn't know I owned and made a glaze for the goose with honey, brandy, and Curaçao. The wild rice she boiled, then crisped in a pan with walnuts and sliced shiitake mushrooms. For a vegetable she had to make do with large carrots, which she sliced and steamed, then covered in a lemon-butter sauce. We drink an entire bottle of Saint-Émilion with the meal. Afterward there's the apple pie and coffee and a thimbleful of Courvoisier.

We are both rosy and sleepy. We put on a CD of Barber's *Adagio for Strings* and take a nap. When I wake up around four-thirty, Gwen is all over me, kissing and rubbing herself against me.

"Jake . . . Jake . . . oh, Jake! I want to make a baby. Right now. Let's make a baby."

"Are you sure?"

"Goddamned right, I'm sure. Let's do it before I change my mind. I've left off the pills for two weeks now. I think my ovaries are ready."

It lasts a long time. When we're finished, we are both exhausted.

"That should have done it—if I didn't burn up all your jism," Gwen says. "I hope it made a little Jacob."

She wants to take a walk and starts hunting around for my spare pair of snowshoes. Spook didn't get much of a run in the drifts this morning when he went out to do his business, so he can use the exercise too.

I give Gwen my good pair of Tubbs shoes, and I use the smaller plastic emergency ones. The snow has slackened, and the sky is beginning to clear. A pale blue is creeping across the heavens from the west. As we walk downtown in the dim light, we watch Spook leap around and plunge into drifts and emerge each time with a fresh dusting of white on his coat. Jody's is closed. She's Catholic. Christmas and Easter Sunday are the only days of the year she doesn't do business. The Antler is open, so we go in to wish everyone a Merry Christmas. Carlton is there and offers to buy us a drink. We quaff a quick beer to be sociable but then make an exit: there's a poker game in progress and the room is roiling with smoke. We walk over to the Bunkhouse and exchange season's greetings with Bob and Bunny. Then we go home. It's seven o'clock, but neither of us is hungry, so we sit before the fire and talk for a while, then I pour each of us a single malt, neat, and go to check my email. There's nothing but a couple of circular end-of-the-year letters from friends in Chicago. Then I think about the pictures of Lila I've got on my hard drive. I haven't purposely kept them secret from Gwen, but knowing she and Lila were friends in the past has probably kept me from telling her. I call to her in the other room.

"I've got some pictures here that might interest you," I say when she comes in. "I forgot to tell you about them before. Somebody left a website address in my mailbox a couple of weeks ago. There were some pictures of Lila."

"Some of the glamour stuff from when she was modeling and in the movies? Let's see them," Gwen says, leaning over my shoulder.

I click up the pictures and run through the first seven. She doesn't say anything. When I get to the tenth, I hear a sharp intake of breath. When I get to twelve, I turn around to see what her reaction has been. She's not there. I get up and go looking. She is in the kitchen, standing with her back against the sink, her empty glass in her hand.

At first I think she's laughing. But when she doesn't look up at me, I realize she is crying.

"Did the pictures upset you that much?"

She looks at me for a second, then her eyes crinkle up and she looks back down. Then she looks back up, tears trickling down her cheeks.

"Goddamn it, Jake. Why did you have to show me those fucking pictures? You know . . . you think you've left something in your past behind. Some part you don't want to remember. But that's not it. It's that you don't want anybody else to know about it. So you hide it from the world, and eventually from yourself. Then when you think it's forgotten somewhere safely behind you, it gets flung in your face, or somebody rubs your nose in it. . . . Where the hell did you get those pictures? I can't believe Lila ever did anything like that. Why would she? She never needed the money. . . .

"There are some things I guess I should have told you about Lila and me. . . . We were close friends for a while, like I told you. But more than that. We were bosom buddies, you might say. . . . Oh, goddamn it."

She turns away toward the window, really weeping now. I don't know whether to go to her or not. She's got to give some signal to indicate what she wants me to do. She sobs for a few minutes, then draws herself up.

"Oh, Jake, I'm sorry . . . I'm sorry. I'd better tell you about this. Can we go in the bedroom? I think I need to lie down."

The only light is from the living room floor lamp, its glow falling across the foot of the bed. We lie down in the half dark.

"I've never told anybody about this. I've needed to get it off my chest for a long time, I guess. But how can you tell. . . . I'll try—I'll try to get it right. It was five—no, four years ago, in the spring of 1995, Lila fell off her horse and wrenched her knee—this much you already know. Lila came to the clinic. She was wearing jeans, which, of course, she had to take off. I was a little nervous and awestruck by Lila's beauty and celebrity. She sat on the table while I examined the knee. It was just some strained ligaments. I felt all around the knee—above, below. She had the most exquisite skin. Her legs were damned near perfect. I guess I blushed while I examined and talked to her, asking what hurt and what didn't. I decided all she needed was a knee brace, which I went into the storage room to get. When I came back, she looked at me with those large hazel eyes and told me I was very attractive. 'I've noticed that before,' she said. 'You could have been a model.'

"While I was kneeling, tightening and adjusting the brace, Lila ran her fingers through my hair. 'Gosh, I wish I had beautiful auburn hair like that. You've got some Indian blood too, don't you? Those fine cheekbones.'

"When I finished adjusting the brace, Lila put her jeans back on, and we stood facing each other.

"Can you come out to the ranch for lunch someday next week? I'd like to see you again when you can slough off the professional manner. It's only a twenty-minute drive. You could take a long lunch break. Olivia fixes divine lunches. What do you say to Wednesday?'

"I said okay. I didn't know what else to say. As she was leaving, she leaned over and pecked me on the cheek. I went to the door and watched her walk over and get in the Jag sedan. I was infatuated. There wasn't anything sexual about it. Maybe underneath. But I didn't want to kiss her lips or embrace her or anything like that. I guess it was more like a schoolgirl crush. Well, I was naïve. I guess after those years in Seattle, I thought I was sophisticated. But I was naïve.

"Are you listening, Jake? I'm trying to tell you something important about my life. I don't think I'm ashamed of what happened later. . . . I know I'm not. But you might not ever feel the same way about me again after I tell you."

"I'm listening."

"I went out to Lila's place that Wednesday. It was a long lunch. Olivia served wonderful blue corn enchiladas with a divine green sauce. Afterward we went up to Lila's room so I could examine Lila's knee to make sure it was healing properly. Lila took off her slacks and sat on the edge of the bed. Then I knelt down and felt her knee. 'It seems to be healing okay,' I said, looking up at her. She wasn't paying attention. She was looking into my eyes. 'You are beautiful, Gwen. Do you mind my saying that?' I shook my head self-consciously. Again she ran her fingers through my hair. Then she leaned down and put her nose against the top of my head and breathed in deeply. My heart started doing wild things. One part of me said to get up and run. But my legs felt like limp noodles—and I didn't run. I knew afterward that I didn't want to run. She pulled me up and kissed me, very gently.

"'Do you like this, Gwen? I think I fell in love with you last week at the clinic. You were so gentle.' She kissed me again and undressed me slowly, murmuring sweet praise for what she was uncovering. And then we made love—but not like that redhead and Lila in the pictures. That first time it was all hands and fingers, and lips, but our lips never went lower than the other's breasts. But, Lord, it was soft and sweet. I had never been so excited in my life. Or since. I wish I could say, 'with present company excepted,' but I can't. Thank God I had gotten Joanna to fill in for me that afternoon, because I didn't get back to Clark City until nine o'clock that night.

"I was in love with Lila and she said she was in love with me. She told me she'd made love to another woman when she was a model, but that was the only time she had wanted another woman until she met me. Lila said she wasn't in love with the other woman anyway—it was just a sexual thing.

"I was really naïve. I wanted to believe her. She made me feel glamorous and sexy and important.

"A few nights later, Lila showed up at my apartment. 'Heah, lovely. I just couldn't stay away,' she said when I opened the door.

"Of course we made love—more passionately than before. I wasn't as uptight. But afterward I told her that I couldn't afford to have her stay overnight. The town folks might catch on, and Clark City wasn't ready for our kind of love. So we made a date to stay in a motel in Great Falls the next weekend.

"Those were two nights of incredible passion. I was entirely worn out physically and emotionally when we drove back in her Jag on Sunday night. But I had never felt so dreamy in all my life.

"It lasted six months. I would go out to the Circle 9 once a week for lunch, when Randal wasn't there—he almost never was—and on most weekends, we would take a trip. We went up to the hotel in East Glacier one weekend, to Big Sky on another. Lila insisted on paying for the rooms—we each took a room although we slept in only one. By the end of a couple of months, we had done nearly everything one woman can do with one another—or so I thought.

"Again, I was wrong. We had gone to Whitefish for the weekend—there was a Texas swing band Lila wanted to hear. When we got ready to go to bed that afternoon, she took a contraption out of her suitcase. A black molded dildo complete with black vinyl harness. She used it on me. I never got to use it on her—I guess it was a dominance thing—but it wouldn't have occurred to me to think of it in those terms. It became a part of our lovemaking from then on. I should have divined that she was more experienced in this Sapphic business than she had allowed. But Christ, I was so immersed in our sensuality I didn't give it a second thought. It was a new excitement. I was in the muck up to my nostrils and I liked it. I didn't want to pull myself out.

"But I started to back off when Lila suggested we enhance our lovemaking with 'helpers,' which I took to mean amphetamines. Lila wanted me to get them from my medical suppliers. That took me aback. I told her I wasn't willing to do that. Not only could I get into big trouble and have my license revoked but I was strongly against using those drugs for 'recreational' purposes. She tried not to show it, but I could tell she was miffed by my puritanical reluctance, so I did give her a number of Zoloft and Prozac tablets when she asked for them later, claiming to be having bouts of depression. But I began to suspect that Lila had had problems with cocaine and maybe stronger drugs in the past. She'd hinted as much in our conversations. It made me step back from our relationship and look at it more objectively. The infatuation was wearing off, but the lovemaking was still terrifically exciting. The surrounding time, however, was beginning to drag. We just didn't have much to say to one another. I don't even remember what we talked about. I just remember she used 'excellent,' 'cool,' 'super,' and 'absolutely,' a lot in our conversations. She never learned to say 'you betcha.'

"What brought the Lila-Gwen affair to an end had nothing to do with drugs. It was a weekend in October, on another of our assignations in Great Falls. I went to Lila's room and was met by Lila and a male visitor, an Air Force colonel, John Bradford, I think his name was. She introduced him and fixed us drinks. Then we began making small talk. It took about twenty minutes for it to penetrate my thick skull that Lila had planned a ménage à trois—and I was expected to be the trois. I was stunned. Then I was pissed. I began to wonder how long she'd been screwing the colonel, all the while pretending to be in love with me. Then I began to see what a joke the whole thing was, and I was the brunt of the joke. I finished my drink, set the glass down on the table, gave them a big smile, and walked out of the room. I went to mine, packed my things, and left the hotel. Fortunately we had driven my Camry. I figured she could get the colonel to take her home. Strangely, I began to feel euphoric. At first I thought it was the result of my having broken off a relationship that had been troubling me for several months. But it was a peculiar euphoria for me, and I realized that Lila had laced my drink with some kind of upper. I began to laugh. I laughed and giggled most of the way back to Clark City.

"Later, after the high had worn off, I wanted to go out to the Circle 9 and whip her ass. But I didn't. In fact I didn't even see her for a couple of months after that. One day around Christmas she came into the post office while I was mailing a package. 'How're you doing, Gwen?' she said, giving me a half smile and a concerned look. You never knew whether those looks were for real or something she'd learned in the modeling and acting business.

"We walked out to the parking lot together, and Lila apologized for the 'fiasco' in Great Falls:

'Relationships never last very long for me. I guess it's the way I'm built.'

"I told her that I had been sore for a while, but I was getting over it and ready to get on with my life. We shook hands. After that we were always cordial with one another, but neither of us tried to fan the spark again.

"You know, I never felt like a lesbian. Of course, after all that sex with Lila, I've thought about sleeping with other women, but I've never met another woman I was attracted to. It was a person-to-person thing, for me at least, not woman to woman. It sure didn't change the way I'm attracted to men. You can vouch for that. It also made me more aware of myself. Parts of me came out that I hadn't known were there. My relationship with Charlie was pretty limited—sexually and emotionally. Lila raised me to a peak, in both ways."

Gwen is quiet for a few moments, but I sense she has more to say, so I stay silent.

"I guess I've been hiding from part of myself since she was killed. I was in love with that woman—deceitful and selfish as she was. I really loved her for a while, and I haven't grieved for her. My weeping in the kitchen was getting some of that out of my system, I guess. Those photographs made me face the fact that she is dead. It wasn't what she was doing with the redhead that bothered me. We'd done all that. . . . After my encounter with the colonel, I figured there was probably a long string of both men and women she'd had relationships with. So I'm not shocked. Or hurt. But finally facing the fact that she is gone forever has been kind of devastating. . . .

"There, Jake. I think I'm okay now. I really did need to get it out of my system. Thanks for listening quietly without interrupting—hey, are you asleep?"

"Asleep!"

"Are you angry? Are you going to throw me over for being a dyke?"

"You were in love with her, weren't you? It was two years before you met me, wasn't it? What should I resent? Besides, how could I throw over the best cook in Montana? That would be improvident."

"Be serious. I need for you to be serious for a little while. Aren't you upset with me?"

"Surprised, I guess, but not upset. Maybe it makes you seem more exotic, more liberated—more complete. I don't know . . . the story sure aroused me. . . . Here, feel."

"What is it with you guys? Why does the lesbian stuff get you so excited? I know men like to look at pictures of women making love. I've seen copies of *Penthouse.* I know you like to fantasize about your women making love to other women, even if you'd never suggest such a thing in reality. But seriously, what is it?"

I tell her the story of Nittaya and Onuma in Bangkok.

"Well, why do you find two pussies engaging each other so sexy?"

"I don't know. I guess guys like to see women in the throes of passion, but they don't want some male surrogate provoking the passion. Maybe it's an outlet for latent homosexuality. I've thought those might be reasons . . . but I know they're not the reason for me."

"Well, what is it?"

"Intimacy. Women must know secrets about each other's bodies, and psyches, both of which are great mysteries for men. It's the kissing that really gets me. . . . The kissing. There's a tenderness in women that is almost alien to men. Women can give themselves up completely to the sexual embrace, which is very difficult for men with their culture-nurtured egos. . . . Christ, I don't really know. I'm just talking."

"Yeah, but I think you're getting close to the truth. Sometimes you do when you just talk about things you haven't thought through before. I've noticed."

She glances down at my still-obvious arousal. "You want to make love again?"

I look at the clock: fifteen minutes to twelve. What a roller-coaster day it has been. I'm physically and emotionally drained. I look at Gwen. She is very mysterious in the half dark.

"You betcha," I say, and begin to take off her clothes. I can't think of a better way to end our Christmas day in this one thousand, nine hundred, and ninety-ninth year of our Lord.

Chapter Seventeen

THIS MORNING GWEN HUSTLES AROUND FROM ROOM TO ROOM straightening and cleaning. She runs the vacuum all over the house. Mops the kitchen and bathroom floors. Moves chairs into new positions. Pulls out shelves of books and dusts them. Everything in the house must be touched and dusted and moved—if only to be put back in its original place. She is preoccupied with something. I guess it's the Lila business that's bothering her.

"You going to talk to me, or are you going to dilly-dally around all day cleaning and rearranging my house?"

"*Our* house."

"*Our* house? Are you moving in permanently?"

"I've thought about it. Last night I found out how broadminded you are. I think I could live with a truly broadminded man as long as he's not too hung up on himself. Besides, we probably made a baby yesterday. I feel like I'm pregnant. Something is going to have to be done about that."

"How can you know you're pregnant the next day?"

"I have this feeling."

"Do you want to get married?"

"Don't get carried away. Maybe I should just live with you . . . and have the baby. Then we can decide about marriage. Marriage is a serious business."

"Having a baby isn't a serious business?"

"Yes, it is, but it's just a natural thing. A woman can have a baby by herself. She just needs the man to get it started."

"Thanks a lot. I'm happy to know I'm needed for something."

"You guys never know, do you?"

"Was your marriage to Charlie a serious business?"

"It was at first, and I guess it got more serious later on. You know we were childhood sweethearts. A hot item in high school. Inseparable in college. Charlie was a year ahead of me in school. When he went to the University of Washington to study international relations, I couldn't wait to join him. I was going to be a biology teacher. He was going to teach social studies. We were both good students. When, during his senior year, he was encouraged by his advisor to continue his program in grad school we decided to get married. Charlie's father ran a hardware store in Wolf Creek for some rich family in Spokane. It was a small store, and he didn't make much money. We agreed that I would finish my degree a semester early by going to summer school, then get a job to support us until he finished his Ph.D. That way he would be able to teach at the college level and we could pay off our educational debts faster.

"At first we were happy, I guess. As happy as twenty-two and twenty-three olds who don't know much about relationships can be. But Charlie was so busy with graduate work he didn't have much time for me, and the deeper he got into his studies, the less time he had. Once I began night classes to ease the boredom, the literature classes I took mixed in with the pre-med made me think about the life of William Carlos Williams. I loved his poetry, or the idea of it—I don't know how much of it I actually understood—and a life as a general practitioner who wrote poems or stories or novels at night when he got home seemed about the perfect life to me.

"I don't know what happened to Charlie. I don't think he was fooling around—if he was, it must have been with a librarian. Maybe he just felt guilty for neglecting me. After the first year we hardly ever made love, and around that time he became verbally abusive. He wasn't the Charlie I had known, or at least thought I had known, all my life. I couldn't do anything right as far as he was concerned. He began to criticize everything I did—my cooking, my housekeeping, the way I dressed. I began to feel bad about myself. One morning he backhanded me across the cheek when I accidentally spilled coffee on one of his research papers. That was it for me. I moved out, got a room in a house with some other girls, and started medical school in earnest.

"I think Charlie was glad to get rid of me. Of course I saw him several times when we were going through the divorce, but after the split I stayed away as much as possible. I haven't seen him since he graduated. He got a job at some small college in Arkansas and is still there as far as I know. When his father died about ten years ago, his mother moved to Cheyenne, where she had family, so I don't have anyone to give me news about his life. I really don't care if I ever hear from him again. I know a lot more about relationships now. I guess the two serious ones I've had—with Charlie and Lila—were pretty destructive. But they taught me a lot about what to look for in a partner. I think I can be happy with you. At least you have a sense of humor."

"Well, ma'am, that is downright flattering. Welcome to *Chez Battle.* Or should we call it *Chez Jefferson-Battle*? Or *Chez Battle-Jefferson*?"

"Jefferson-Battle sounds better. Let's make it that—unless we get married. Then it can be just Battle. I'm old-fashioned. And I know a Virginian wouldn't have it any other way, even if my name is Jefferson."

It's a good conversation, and it gets Gwen's mind off cleaning the house. By mid-afternoon I've convinced her to sit down in the living room in front of the fire and read *The Captain's Daughter* while I work on my novel. It's eight o'clock before we call it quits. She cooks a Provençal-style *omelette aux champignons* for supper, then we go to bed. Gwen falls asleep almost immediately. As I lie there listening to her soft, even breathing, a warm languor creeps up my body and diffuses my mind. Drifting off to sleep, I try to remember if I've ever felt so contented at any other time since childhood.

This morning I walk Gwen to the clinic, then go back home to work on the novel, which recently has come to a standstill. About ten-thirty Ralston calls to see if anything happened over the holiday that might shed light on the murder. No, I tell him. He says no one has come up with an ID on the fingerprints either. I hang up and go back to work. At noon I decide to go see Carlton and discuss some plans for dealing with Goon if he shows up in town. I find Carlton at the Bunkhouse, lying on his bed reading a Tony Hillerman novel.

"What's up, Jake?"

"Let's go over to the Antler and get a beer and some lunch. I want to talk strategy on dealing with Buck Wallace and Goon."

We've just been served our sandwiches when Nerice hands me the phone.

"It's Gwen. She sounds really upset."

"Jake . . . oh, Jake. That damned Goon just shot Spook."

"Where are you?"

"At your house. Come quick."

When Carlton and I get there, Gwen has Spook laid out on the bed. She's examining and doctoring his wound—not very well. She is weeping uncontrollably but manages to tell me that she'd come home at lunchtime to walk Spook. But just as she stepped in the kitchen, she heard shouting—something unintelligible—from the backyard.

"I didn't know who it was. When I opened the back door, he yelled, 'You ugly beech . . . I kill you good.' Oh, Jake, that son of a bitch tried to shoot me. He opened fire with a little machine gun that looked like a toy. Bullets were flying everywhere. Look around the walls in the kitchen. I don't know how he missed me. Spook ran through the door so fast I didn't have time to stop him. He flew off the back porch right at Goon. I guess one of the bullets hit him before he got on the man, because when Spook clamped down on his arm, Goon went crazy. He dropped the gun and was swinging Spook around trying to throw him off like he was terrified, shaking and dancing around in the snow."

Finally Spook let go, and Goon went running off toward the school. By that time Gwen had managed to get her .25 out of her purse. She emptied the clip, all six shots, at him but doesn't know whether she hit him—he was pretty far away and just kept running.

"We've got to get Spook to Dr. Johnson in Great Falls," she says. "I don't know how badly he's hurt. The bullet went through his lower abdomen. I can't tell whether it hit anything vital. He doesn't seem to be in much pain, and I don't want to give him morphine. . . ."

Telling me the story has calmed her down somewhat. I look at Spook. He seems alert but like he knows he's injured. The bullet's entry and exit holes are small, so it didn't mushroom when it hit him.

Carlton comes in from the backyard with Goon's gun. It's a Bizon 2, the 9 mm. A nasty little weapon. The magazine is still half full. There are holes in the door and in the kitchen wall behind where Gwen was standing. I'd hung a print of Gauguin's *Two Tahitian Women with Mango Blossoms* over the kitchen table; both women have holes in their chests. How the Goon missed Gwen astounds me.

By this time half of Clark City is in my house or standing in the front yard. I give Tim Free my .44-40 and send him off tracking to see if he can find out where Goon went. Then I ask Gus Fox to get the ambulance and drive Gwen and Spook to Great Falls. I've decided I've got to force matters with Buck Wallace. I tell Carlton to get his weapons—we're going out to the Circle 9.

"Don't go out there, Jake," Gwen begs me. "That Goon is too dangerous. Get Ralston to go with you at least."

"It would take him a couple of hours to get there. I can't wait that long. Nevertheless, I call Ralston's office and leave a message, explaining what has happened in the couple of hours since I spoke with him. Then Carlton and I dig the 4Runner out of the snow and get it started. Just as we pull into the street, Gus arrives with the ambulance. Bob Taylor and Phil Turner are carrying Spook out of the house on a blanket with Gwen leading the way. Just as I turn the corner, Tim Free comes running up.

"His tracks led over to the school parking lot, Jake. He must have gotten in a car there. I don't know where he went. There's no one around the school to ask if they saw him. . . . Where are you two headed?"

"Turrentine's ranch. I'm going to get Buck Wallace to give me some answers."

"You want me to go with you?"

"You'd better stay here. The Goon may still be around. Shoot the bastard on sight if you see him. There's no telling what kind of arsenal he has."

When we pull up at Turrentine's house, I scan the vehicles in the parking lot. The Land Rover is there, which means Buck retrieved it from the Great Falls police. The GMC pickup and the Ford Super 350 are there as well. The Ford has a snow blade installed, and the drive, the parking lot, and the landing strip have been cleared of snow. There is no plane out on the strip. When we pass the garage, I check to see that the Jaguar is in its bay.

"Okay, Carlton. Goon probably isn't here. Maybe Buck isn't either, since the Yukon is missing. But both of them could be."

I tell Carlton to take his .270 and stand by a nearby cottonwood, where he should have a pretty good shot at whoever answers the door.

"Got you covered, Jake. Just be careful."

I've got my .38 loose under my coat in the shoulder holster, and I stand a little to the right of the door when I ring the bell. I ring twice before Buck opens the door.

"What do you want, Mr. Battle? You know Mr. Turrentine isn't here."

"I've come out to see you, Buck. I need answers to some questions about Dimitri Sulamanov and the drug business you and he and Lila were running."

I don't know if Buck can see Carlton or not, but he takes a quick step back so he's out of Carlton's line of vision and starts to go for his gun. He'll have the drop on me—I know I can't get my .38 out in time—so I lunge through the door and catch him with my forearm just before he lifts the gun free of his shoulder holster. When I slam him into the wall of the foyer, my elbow catches his Adam's apple and he squawks like a raven. As he rebounds off the wall, I bring my knee up in his crotch. He grunts, sags, and slides to the floor. I have hold of his right wrist, but I know he's let go of the gun. I reach inside his coat and pull the weapon out of his holster. It's a .357 Colt Trooper. I cock it and hold it against his temple while I frisk him. My gun hand is shaking badly.

"He try to shoot you, Jake?"

Carlton is standing in the doorway behind me with his .270 pointed at Buck.

"He was going for this cannon. I crushed him against the wall."

Buck gazes up at me, his eyes looking as if he can't quite break through to consciousness.

"First question, Buck. Is that Goon Dimitri here at the house? Answer quick, I don't want to have to kick you again."

Buck doesn't try to talk, just shakes his head no.

"Do you know where he is?"

Again a head shake—no.

"Can I do anything to help, Mr. Battle?"

It's Jeremy, standing in the doorway to the living room. I catch a glimpse of Olivia peeking out from behind him.

"No, Jeremy. . . . Have you seen the big guy in the last couple of days?"

"He was here yesterday morning. He took the station wagon. I haven't seen him since."

"How did he get here? There's no plane on the strip."

"I don't know, Mr. Battle. He just appeared."

"A friend brought him out from Great Falls," Buck croaks.

His eyes have cleared, but he doesn't try to move.

"Your friend or his?"

"His. Alfred. He's a dealer. I don't know his last name. I saw him only a couple of times when I rode in with Mrs. Turrentine."

"Delivering cocaine?"

Buck nods his head, yes.

"Okay, Buck. Let's go in the living room. I've got a lot more questions to ask."

I tell Carlton to take a position by the front window in the dining room where he can see the driveway and walk and ask Jeremy to cover the back door.

"Can you use a gun?"

"Yes, sir. I suppose I can."

I hand him Buck's .357 and show him how it works. Then I help Buck up, haul him into the living room, and sit him on the couch. I sit in a lounge chair across from him and take out my notebook. He looks a little more alert.

"Okay, Buck. We know you were mixed up in this drug mess with Lila and the Goon. And you knew about Lila's murder. You knew that Goon shot her and you didn't give him up. That makes you an accessory, and unless you cooperate from now on, Ralston Nichols is going to string you up by your balls. Turrentine knows you were involved—Sheriff Nichols and I told him last week. Goon tried to kill Gwen Jefferson earlier this afternoon at my house. How he missed her, I don't know. But I'm mad as hell and I'm going to get the story out of you if I have to beat it out with a poker. . . . Do you understand?"

Buck says he's willing to cooperate and would have come forward earlier but is terrified of Goon.

"The guy is crazy, Mr. Battle. Real crazy. Several times I've thought he was going to shoot me or tear me apart with his hands. Once I saw him rip the fender off a truck."

Buck says he didn't want to get mixed up in the drug business with Lila, but she threatened to tell her husband he'd raped her if he didn't play along. If she got caught with the junk, she was going to tell the police that Buck was the one who was the connection. She knew he had a record and had been suspected of drug trafficking in Houston.

Buck not only talks, he seems to want to talk. Maybe he figures that's the only way he can rid himself of Goon. During the next hour I get a pretty complete account of what's happened over the past several years.

When Turrentine bought the ranch in 1992 and was looking for someone to oversee his interests there, Buck asked for the job. He felt burned out as head of security at Club Diablo in Houston and was also afraid the police were hot on his trail as a dealer—or the overseer of dealers–in drugs. Turrentine gave him the job and charged him with keeping Lila under control. Turrentine didn't want to restrict her activities too severely, so he knew it would be impossible to keep her away from dealers in Great Falls and Helena. Buck was supposed to keep an eye on her and make sure she didn't stray too far—at least not so far as to get herself in trouble. It seemed an easy enough job—at least the air was clean in Montana.

"Houston had gotten so bad that I was glad to be out of there. The business was becoming too risky. A lot of people were involved—some of them not so smart. I never liked the coke dealing anyway, but being security at the club, I had to oversee what was going on. People came to Club Diablo because they knew coke and amphetamines were available anytime they wanted them—not from us, but from the slinks who hung around the club. . . . It wasn't just the club that bothered me. All the rackets in Houston were getting nasty—everybody was getting too greedy. It seemed even legitimate business was beginning to stink. I snatched up this job when I had the chance. I thought I'd be able to breathe easier in these wide open spaces."

For a few years Lila had surprised them all and kept a rein on herself. As far as Buck knew, she stayed clean until the winter of

1995. But something must have happened about that time because her moods began to change. She seemed to be depressed a lot. Then he noticed signs that she'd started using again. For days at a time she'd stay in her suite upstairs and have her food carried up to her. Usually Olivia brought the trays down with the food just picked over. Sometimes when Lila came downstairs, her eyes were glazed and she'd smile dreamily, as if her mind was living somewhere else.

Then she'd straighten out for months. She expended a lot of energy horseback riding, often obsessively, five or six hours a day. Other times she went into Clark City socializing. Buck kept Randal informed about her habits—when she was using and when she wasn't. If Buck thought she was losing control, Randal would visit the ranch, sometimes for as long as a month. In that way they kept Lila in check. Then, in October, just over a year ago, Goon drove up one day. Buck had never seen him before. Lila took him out to the landing strip and when he left, she led Buck out to the guesthouse and explained what she and Goon had planned. Her dealer in Great Falls had put Lila and Goon in touch. Buck learned that Goon flew sizable shipments from some cartel in Mexico into Texas, New Mexico, and Arizona. Then he'd fly parcels to places along the Rocky Mountains like Tucson, Denver, Fort Collins, Cheyenne, Salt Lake, Butte, and Great Falls. Using the Turrentine airstrip, he could avoid the danger of exposing himself at public airports and makeshift airstrips that the feds knew about.

That day in the guesthouse Lila threatened Buck, blackmailing him into keeping quiet about the fly-ins. She started paying him a share of the profits to involve him more and ensure he wouldn't go to the police or tell Turrentine. Goon would fly in a shipment; Buck and Lila would then take the coke to Great Falls, and sometimes Butte. Everything went smoothly for a year, until this Alfred in Great Falls learned that the feds were suspicious of fly-ins along the Rocky Mountain front. He heard that they didn't know who was involved or where they landed but special agents had been sent in to investigate. He warned Dimitri, who told Lila they'd have to stop flying to the ranch until the heat was off. That upset her. Buck didn't know why at first. She never needed the money, and she had plenty of contacts in Butte and Great Falls to feed her habit. There was something about her relationship with Dimitri—something Buck hadn't understood. He says that the three of them met here in the house one day and Lila proposed that instead of flying the shipments to the ranch, they could make drops over in the wilderness at Golden Meadows. She suggested they might even land the plane on the prairie, it was so flat. Lila rode her horse in the area fairly often. She could be there when Dimitri made a drop and bring the shipment in on a packhorse.

Buck told her the idea was impractical. The Forest Service would be on them in a minute for bringing a plane into a motor-restricted area. Goon started shouting that she was crazy and wanted to get him killed. Then she started shouting at Goon that he was ruining her life. Buck stayed out of the argument. Finally, Goon gave in and agreed to go out for a look, but that was all he was going for—a look.

Lila put the two horses in the trailer and drove over to Benchmark, where Buck and Goon had agreed to meet her. Buck thought Lila and Goon would ride out, look the place over, then come right back. He waited nearly four hours at the outfitters' corral before Goon came back with the two horses but without Lila. He told Buck that Lila had tried to kill him with her pistol. She hit him in the thigh and left shoulder, but he was able to get the rifle out of the scabbard and shoot her. He thought maybe her gun had jammed before she could get off another shot.

"The more he talked about how Lila had suckered him out to the wilderness, the madder he got," Buck says.

Afraid that Dimitri might try to kill him as well, Buck assured Goon he had no idea what Lila was planning. In an attempt to divert the Goon's ire, he explained how they could make Carlton seem to be the murderer, since Buck knew that Carlton had been Lila's lover and it was Carlton's gun that had killed her. He also promised Dimitri he would drive to Great Falls and tell Alfred what had happened, so the dealer would be ready to provide Dimitri with a car to get him safely into Canada. He could also get a doctor to see to Dimitri's wounds (flesh wounds he seemed to mind no more than mosquito bites).

"How did Dimitri get Carlton's rifle?"

"I gave it to him. He was scared to death of animals—except for horses. He seemed to like horses. Often he rode with Mrs. Turrentine when he was here. He especially liked that big cavalry horse, Major, but other animals, all kinds of animals, he despised—even dogs and cats. He wouldn't let Soshie, Mrs. Turrentine's Afghan wolfhound, or Olivia's two cats near him. Imagine a big ugly guy like that afraid of cats. He'd heard there were bears and cougars in the wilderness, and he was as frightened as a child. He insisted on taking a rifle instead of a pistol, so I gave him Carlton's—I didn't want him using one of Mr. Turrentine's Weatherby Magnums. He also took a big knife, about the size of a bayonet."

"That was convenient, your having Carlton's gun. When did you steal it?"

"Yeah . . . I stole it from his room in the Bunkhouse. I'd heard about it at the Antler—people ribbed him about it. I knew his door would be unlocked. . . .

"When I found out Carlton was screwing Mrs. Turrentine, I got nervous. I was afraid he'd find out about our operation and turn us in, he seemed such a straight arrow. I guess I was angry too. I didn't like the idea of a greasy Indian making it with her. I never did like that guy. I was going to fix him somehow. But I never figured out what to do with that rifle. I would never have shot Mrs. Turrentine. I did think about shooting Carlton with his own gun, though, and making it look like an accident. But I couldn't decide on a plan. The rifle was in my closet when Dimitri wanted a gun, so I gave it to him. When Dimitri came back from Golden Meadows with both the rifle and Lila's pistol, I knew they were bound to have Goon's prints all over them, so I threw them into Nilan Reservoir on my way to town."

"But why would Lila want to kill the Goon?" I ask him. "That just doesn't make sense. He wasn't threatening her, was he?"

"I think it was something else. Something personal. But I don't know what it was."

"Was there more between them than the cocaine?"

"Yeah, it was weird. She was a beautiful woman and he was the ugliest man I ever saw outside a freak show. But she seemed to find him fascinating. She'd play up to him, then she'd get mad and pretend she didn't want to have anything to do with him—like a little kid. I never saw her act like that with anybody else. One evening I was making the rounds, checking the cars and buildings like I did every night. Dimitri had been staying in the guesthouse for several days. It was summer and the window was up when I passed his room, the shade was raised about a third of the way, and the light was on. There they were—stark naked—going at it like two dogs. Mrs. Turrentine was bent over the bed and he was shoved up behind her. She was saying, 'Bet, Bet, Bet, oh, Bet' over and over, like a chant. And he was grunting and saying something like, 'Bee-Let, I fuck you good. I fuck you good.' Then he said something in that language of his. She kept calling him Bet, or Bat. He called her Bee-Let, or Bee-Lat—it was always hard for me to tell what he said. I guess they were screwy nicknames they had for each other. I watched for a while—I wanted to walk away but I couldn't. When he came, I thought he'd tear her up he went so crazy. But she seemed to like the battering. When he pulled out, she flipped over and took his big cock in her mouth and sucked him out. It was disgusting, one of the most disgusting things I've ever seen. I thought I was going to vomit. . . . I never spied on them after that. But I think they went at it whenever Dimitri was staying at the ranch, and that sometimes Lila met him in Great Falls. . . . *Hay-soos*, that Dimitri is scarier than anything I had to deal with in New Orleans or Houston."

"After all that, why do you think he came back? Lila was dead, the drug operation was finished. What reason could he have had to hang around? Do you think he'll come back today?"

"I never know when he's coming back or what he's doing. He just arrives in the plane or in a car. Usually he takes the Yukon if he wants to go somewhere. I've never tried to stop him. He has his own key—I guess he had one made. Or maybe Mrs. Turrentine gave him one. When he showed up yesterday, he came in to ask me if the feds had been out to check the airstrip. Then he jumped in the Yukon and took off. . . . I don't know why he's hanging around either. If I were him, I'd be off to Canada or Mexico knowing the law is bound to be after him. . . . Maybe he thinks he can keep on using the airstrip if the feds haven't been investigating it."

"But that doesn't explain why he called Gwen on the phone, and why he threatened her and me and why he tried to kill her."

"I don't know Mr. Battle. He's a screwy guy. He seemed to have a grudge against a lot of people. Even Mr. Turrentine. I heard him tell Mrs. Turrentine that her husband was in for a lot of trouble. He didn't say why and she didn't seem to care. I just don't know why she tried to kill him, or why he would want to kill Miss Jefferson."

"If he does come back to establish the airstrip as a base of operations or for any other reason and you've vacated the premises he's going to know something is up. . . . I want to make a deal with you—if I can get Sheriff Nichols to okay it. I want you to stay at the ranch. Pretend I've never been here. If the Goon shows up, call me immediately. Or get Jeremy to call me. I'll figure some way to get here and take him out without endangering you or Jeremy and Olivia. We can park my 4Runner down below that grove of aspens, then Carlton and Tim Free and I can sneak up here and try to get him when his guard is down. The police don't have any evidence about the drug running, so it's likely you can escape prosecution for that. If you help us get Goon, I'm pretty sure the accessory-to-murder charge can be overlooked as well. You and Turrentine can decide how to square relations between the two of you. Is it a deal? Or do you want to face a lengthy Montana incarceration?"

Buck agrees, so I call Helena to see if Ralston is on his way to the ranch. Barney says he left about an hour ago. I call Phil Turner at the Antler and tell him to get Tim Free or Gus Fox to wave down Ralston when he comes through town and to have him call me at the Circle 9. Half an hour later the phone rings. Jeremy answers: it's Ralston. I tell him what I've found out from Buck and explain the deal I want to make.

"I got no objections, Jake. I guess that's the only way we're going to catch that son of a bitch. Nobody here has seen him since he shot at Gwen, but Janie over at the restaurant saw Turrentine's Yukon leaving town on the Simms highway about two this afternoon. I guess he was headed for Great Falls. I've already put out an APB on the Yukon. Maybe we can nail this Dimitri before he causes any more trouble. . . . Before you hang up, Phil wants to relay a message from Gwen."

Phil tells me Gwen called from the veterinary hospital in Great Falls. Spook is in a bad way. Dr. Johnson cut out about a foot of intestine that was torn up pretty badly. The doc says that with the antibiotics and Spook being a strong dog, he may make it. But he may not.

"But let me tell you, that dog is a hero here in Clark City. If he dies we're going to build a memorial. If he hadn't gotten to that guy when he did, Gwen would have been cut to pieces. We counted six holes in the door and nine in the kitchen wall. Forty-five rounds were left in the magazine. It's a good thing Spook jumped him when he did. . . . I've always thought that dog was half human."

Tim Free is there with Gwen when I get home. She's still visibly shaken. She wants me to look at all the bullet holes in the kitchen plaster. She's crying and keeps saying, "I don't see how he missed me. You'd think at least a couple of them would have had to go through me to hit the wall where they did."

Tim is sitting near the front door with my .44-40 across his lap. He says that several bullets had ricocheted off the door and the jamb.

"That's why it looks like he covered the whole wall. Those little machine pistols are hard to aim and control. I shot an Uzi once. I couldn't hit shit. The bullets just fly everywhere. I think you're supposed to scare your enemy to death. . . . But at that range, I don't see how he missed either. I guess the Powers were protecting our little Miss Gwenie Nightingale. If it hadn't been for that dog. . . ."

Gwen starts crying again.

Tim gets up, hands me the rifle, and says he's going home. He just wanted to keep Gwen company until I got back.

I try to comfort her: "Spook is a strong dog who doesn't want to die. We'll just have to have faith in his power to heal himself."

Later I let her know what Buck Wallace told me. Without recounting the details, I tell her he'd seen Lila and the Goon getting it on together.

"Jesus, Jake, how could she fuck that ugly bastard? It makes me clam up just thinking about him."

"I don't know. Ask Lamont Cranston. . . ."

"Be serious, Jake. Remember she was special to me for a while. And I'm still shook up and worried sick about Spook. I don't feel like 'funny' right now."

"I'm sorry. I guess I'm just trying to dissipate the gloom."

Neither of us is hungry. We drink a single malt on the rocks, then go to bed. Gwen snores quietly for a few minutes, then sinks into slow, even breathing. As I drift in and out of sleep, images of Dimitri Sulamanov rise and fade in my brain. Even though I've never seen him, I think I know exactly how he looks. Strangely, his eyes are sadder than a dog's. They stare at me out of his pathetically disfigured face.

"You shoot me," he says in a quiet, childlike voice. "You shoot me, I shoot you."

One morning Captain Stevenson sends my platoon up a creek bed on the northeast slope of Hill 937 (Dong Ap Bia—the Mountain of the Crouching Beasts, the Viets call it). My orders are to make contact with the enemy and mark the location of his fortifications. I have my men fan out and move cautiously behind me. We're looking into the trees as well as along the ground. There will be snipers. I've never seen such thick bamboo and vines. We have to force our way through with machetes and bayonets until we get to the wash. Aerial intelligence says we'll find bunkers and caves about fifteen hundred meters from our jump-off point. We've advanced about seven hundred meters without a sign of Charlie when all hell breaks loose. From some point up the wash, AK-47s begin spraying our formation. Rocket grenades are bouncing off trees and exploding around us. I'm on point, thirty meters ahead of the forward line of our men. There's a jam of uprooted palms twenty meters up the wash. I slither in behind the trees and look back for casualties. The men are caught in the open but partially shielded by the height of the logjam. I signal for them to fall back behind a natural berm on the left. Only Severance is being carried. When they're safely behind the berm, I crawl farther in among the palm trunks until I can see up the wash. The firing has ceased and now there is only the crepuscular jungle silence that puts your nerves on edge. The foliage is dense ahead of me, and I can't see any bunkers. I've trained myself to detect them—there's always some disturbance of the natural order. Often I couldn't tell you what it was—an instinct, a sixth sense. As I scan the terrain I notice movement, at first as if the forest itself is creeping forward. Then the crouched forms of ten or twelve NVA soldiers spread out across the stream bed. They're forty or fifty meters away, but my platoon can't see them because of the logjam. My men lob several rifle grenades over the jam and fire randomly up the wash. I pick the gooks off, one at a time. K-chat, I see him fall. K-chat, another. The others look wildly about. They can't locate my position. K-chat, another. K-chat, another. The rest hit the ground. I spot a pith helmet. K-chat. Four or five AKs open up on my log pile. I bury myself behind a big bole. Two minutes, by my watch. I look over the log. A gook is advancing cautiously; he's twenty meters away. K-chat. Three rush my log fort. K-chat, k-chat, k-chat, k-chat, k-chat, k-chat. . . . My M-16 jams. There's one gook left standing, ten meters away. He lifts his AK-47 and fires. The rounds zip by close above my head. Then one tears through the fabric of my fatigues and plows a furrow across my upper right arm. There's no time to draw my .45, so I roll to the left and pull out my survival knife. He leaps on the log above me and swings his muzzle down. It's like slow motion. I stare at his toes, poking out the end of his sandals. They're deformed with calluses, the nails jutting out at odd angles. I don't want to die, but if I'm going to, I'm taking this *gook with me. My knife comes up of its own volition and slashes his Achilles tendon. I roll to the right just as he fires a burst into the ground. His knees buckle and he falls into the mud beside me. My knife slices through his jugular and rips his windpipe. Blood spurts all over my face. I can't see his eyes. I wipe the blood from my brow and eyes and look up the wash. Another NVA soldier is running toward me. He fires his AK-47 wildly, splintering logs to my left. I rip out my .45, duck down behind the big bole and roll onto my back. When his upper body rises into view, I point and fire. He's only three meters away. I can see directly into his eyes. There is no fear, no anger—only surprise. The big 230-grain slug catches him in the breastbone and stands him up for a moment. Then he collapses, as if all the bones in his body have suddenly dissolved.*

I'm shaking uncontrollably from the adrenaline rush, high as a U-2 spy plane. It's begun to drizzle. The cool mist on my face is a welcome relief. I wait for my blood to dissipate a little of the excitement. Then I wave the platoon forward and send Begay and Wells up the draw to check for gook survivors. Severance has a hole in his thigh, but the slug missed the bone. Hayduke treats and bandages the wound before we put Severance and Young in a good defensive position behind the logjam and tell them to make sure it isn't us on the way back before they shoot. Then Hayduke rips off what's left of the sleeve of my fatigues and looks at the furrow the slug plowed across my arm.

"Too bad, Lieutenant. Not serious enough to buy you a ticket home." He cleans the wound, dresses it, and gives me a shot of antibiotic. When Begay and Wells get back to report all clear, I don't ask any questions but order the platoon up the draw, putting Lawson on point; he has an uncanny ability to detect mines. We find the bunkers one click to the southwest. We crawl within a hundred meters in good cover. Ahead is a cleared area to give the enemy machine gunners unobstructed lines of fire. Even the elephant grass has been clipped to knee height. Captain Stevenson's orders from Colonel Honeycutt were to locate and mark the bunkers on the map. We are not to attack. I study the emplacements and write down the coordinates. Then I tell Belen to stay with me and send the rest of the platoon back down the wash. Belen has the M-79 grenade launcher and he is very good with it.

"Don't mention this when we get back to Battalion, Belen. . . . Put a round through that embrasure."

He puts three grenades into the bunker before we retreat down the draw to catch up with the platoon. The rain has started to come down hard now. Water is already running five inches deep in the wash. The heavy drops trickle over my skin, bathing away the encrusted sweat. As we move down the creek, the post-adrenal euphoria begins to creep up my fingers and toes. . . . Goon is still looking at me with his sad, doglike eyes, awaiting my answer: "I'm ready whenever you are, big guy."

Chapter Eighteen

Yesterday when I called the ranch to talk with Buck Wallace, Jeremy answered the phone.

"Mr. Buck's out in the pickup making sure the airstrip is clear. . . . No, sir, we haven't seen hide nor hair of Mr. Dimitri. I guess he thought he'd better get out of the country after shooting at Miss Jefferson. Is she all right?"

I tell him Gwen is fine but her dog is still in critical condition.

"Jeremy, are you and Olivia all right? Do you mind staying out there? Dimitri might know something was up if he came back and you and Olivia had disappeared."

"We're fine. Mr. Turrentine called from Houston and said he'd be back at the ranch by Wednesday morning. We'll all be fine once he gets here . . . except Mr. Buck. I kind of wonder what Mr. Turrentine is going to say to him about the drug business. I'll make sure Mr. Turrentine knows that Mr. Dimitri has been around. Once they're back, Modell can handle things out here."

I felt Gwen was safe this morning. Yesterday we'd taken my .44-40 and .44 Magnum over to the clinic and stored them out of sight—but readily accessible—just in case. Gwen knows how to use a gun; she learned to shoot as a child and is a crack shot. I went over to check on her several times yesterday and this morning. I would have stayed and worked in one of the examining rooms, but she wouldn't let me. Tim Free volunteered to patrol the town every couple of hours, so I came home and tried to take my mind off Goon by working on the novel. I'm at it again this afternoon when Randal Turrentine calls.

"Jake, I flew in this morning. Buck has filled me in. I can understand how Lila coerced him into keeping quiet about the drug smuggling, but I'll never forgive him for not telling me about this Dimitri fellow. . . . I guess he was scared stiff by the man. He tells me that Dimitri and Lila had a thing going. That woman never ceases to amaze me—even from the land of the dead. I'll bet she's putting the make on Lucifer right now. I think it had something to do with her father, but I could never get her to talk about it."

I listen, thinking what a smooth talker Turrentine is, delivering his spiel as if it was a prepared speech for a board of directors' meeting.

"Things are under control out here. Modell has mobilized the troops. Scott Dawkins is armed to the nines. He knows a lot about ambush—had plenty of experience with the Contras. Buck is trying to redeem himself by scouting the area every hour. We've even got Jeremy and Olivia on the lookout. My secretary, Iris Stoop, is also carrying a .38. We can take care of ourselves, unless this Dimitri shows up with an army. . . . Why do you suppose that guy is hanging around Clark City anyway? I think I'd be trying to put as much distance between Clark City and myself as possible if I'd made as many enemies in the area as he has."

"I don't know. Doesn't make much sense, does it? There's that old proverb about the scene of the crime. . . . Anyway, if he does come back, let me know immediately."

"I'm sorry about Miss Jefferson. I imagine this Dimitri scared her pretty bad, but I'm happy she wasn't hurt. I wouldn't want *anybody* in Clark City to suffer because of Lila and all our trouble. . . . If there's anything I can do for you and Miss Jefferson, you just let me know. I'll be staying here until about the tenth, trying to settle my affairs in Montana. I'll probably put the ranch on the market this spring. I've no use for it now that Lila is gone."

It sounds like Turrentine has the ranch secure as a fortress and I won't need to worry about them anymore—I'll just have to see to the safety of Clark City.

This evening Gwen comes home worn out. Patients have streamed into the clinic all day. She's particularly upset about a boy who slipped off a snow-covered cattle-loading ramp. His head hit a concrete stanchion. He has a serious concussion as well as a broken left arm. Gwen set the arm and put ten stitches in the boy's forehead, then got Gus Fox to drive him to the hospital in Great Falls.

"Ranching can be dangerous business, Jake. My brother Tom was nearly killed by a bull that ran over him when he was about the same age as this kid."

When we go in the kitchen to cook supper, Gwen says, "We've got to get those bullet holes patched. It gives me the willies to look at them. I just think of Spook. . . . I called Dr. Johnson this morning. He said Spook was in a coma but his life signs were fairly strong. I'm going in to Great Falls early tomorrow and wait to open the clinic when I get back around eleven."

I promise to get Carlton to fix the wall, and to put some wood putty in the door facing and paint over it. But maybe I'll just take the time and fix it myself.

"I don't want to be reminded of that scare," she says. "Did I tell you I wet my pants? Soaked them! Thank God I changed them before the whole town got over here. Else I would have had to wear them into Great Falls. . . ."

Tonight when Gwen gets home from the clinic, I can tell she is upset again, so I give her a drink and wait for her to unburden herself. We get all the way through supper without her looking at me except for a glance now and then. She picks over the food and leaves her plate three-quarters full. Finally she tells me she doesn't think Spook is going to make it.

"He didn't look so good when I saw him this morning. I held his head and rubbed his ears, but he never opened his eyes."

"What did Dr. Johnson say?"

"That you could never tell with animals. They're like people. Sometimes they come back strong just when you're afraid they're going to give up the ghost. He's doing all he can and trying to keep my hopes up."

I suggest coffee and maybe a piece of pie, but she shakes her head.

"I'm tired, Jake. Maybe I ought to take a pill and go to bed."

"A pill? What is it, Gwen? It's more than *tired*."

"Thanks for patching the wall and door. . . . What are you going to do about that Gauguin print?"

She knows it's one of my favorite paintings.

"I saved the frame. I'll order another print from the Metropolitan. I'd hate to go the rest of my life without those two women close by—they've assumed a presence in my psyche. But that's not getting us any closer to what's bothering you. It's more than Spook, isn't it? Are you going to tell me or not?"

"Let's go in the bedroom. I'm too tired to sit at the table."

She lies on the bed and I sit on the edge beside her. In the dim light she tells her tale.

"Remember a couple of weeks ago I told you about Naomi Winslow taking care of the Turrentine horses? I told you I'd ask her if she'd noticed anything unusual at the ranch that might shed some light on Lila's murder. After you found out about Goon from Jeremy, I felt that Naomi probably couldn't add anything important. Besides, I hadn't seen her in over a month. This afternoon she appeared at the clinic—she'd come down with the flu and wanted some medicine and advice. While I was examining her, I asked if she was still caring for the horses. She said she hadn't been since Lila's murder. Her mother had told her she shouldn't. She had already taught Buck and Olivia how to feed and care for the horses so they could fill in for her when she was away. But yesterday Mr. Turrentine had called, asking how much he owed her. She told him she didn't want any more money, since she had called Buck right after Thanksgiving and told him she was giving up the job. He said he was sending her a thousand dollars anyway for her education fund. Then he said he wanted her to have Scheherazade, Lila's little Arabian mare, to remember her by. He was going to sell the rest of the horses. When she told me that, she began to cry. Just tears at first, but then she began to sob.

" 'What's the matter, honey? Are you so upset about Lila's death? Were you close friends?'

" 'Yes, ma'am. I liked her a lot. . . .'

"Then she started weeping uncontrollably. She's a strong girl. Maybe she could have controlled herself if she hadn't been sick. But maybe it was good for her to get it all out. Her mother and father are exemplary Montana stoics. I was sure she couldn't let herself go at home. I wanted to hug her, but I couldn't without being awkward because she was sitting on the examining table, so I just held her hand and let her cry. After she quiets down, she lifts her head: 'I didn't mean to come all to pieces. I haven't been able to talk to mama—it would kill her.'

"What would kill her? I asked myself. Then it began to penetrate my thick skull. I felt my blood chill. My forehead and hands got clammy. My God, I thought, do you suppose Lila told her about us? So I asked if she wanted to talk about it: 'There are no patients waiting. I can listen.'

"'Yes, ma'am. I don't know who else to talk to. I've been scared a long time. You being a doctor, maybe you could tell me some things I don't know. But you won't tell mama, will you?'

"'Of course not. You tell me anything you need to get off your mind. It will be just between the two of us.'

"Naomi is an attractive girl. Not pretty. More tomboyish with her hair cut short. But she's just a kid—only seventeen years old.

When she began to tell her story, she spoke in a quiet voice, looking up at me occasionally but mostly with her eyes downcast. Naomi said Lila had been friendly with her from the beginning—for the three years she'd been caring for the horses. Lila would invite her to the house for a Coke or a cup of coffee and a snack when Naomi came over after school. She found she could talk to Lila in a way she couldn't with anyone else, so she had spoken a lot about herself—her school activities, her 4-H projects, her boyfriends, her ambitions. Lila always listened with interest. Then she would tell Naomi stories about New York and Paris, Milan and Hollywood. In that way they had become close.

"From what Naomi told me, I guessed that she'd developed an intense crush on Lila. I could relate to that. Anyway, last summer after the county schools were closed, Lila had asked Naomi to come to the ranch early some afternoons to go riding with her. They would start off at two or three o'clock and ride until six or seven in the evening. Sometimes Naomi stayed over for dinner after calling her mother to make sure it was okay. Naomi had learned to relax around Lila. She told me she felt pretty much at home on the ranch. One afternoon in August she went riding with Lila in the woods on the west side of the ranch where the creek comes down out of the foothills. It was a hot day. Lila suggested they stop at a big pool she knew farther up the creek and go swimming to cool off. They unsaddled and unbridled their horses to let them graze. Then they went down to the creek. Naomi thought they'd go swimming in their underpants and bras, but Lila took off everything.

"As I listened to Naomi recall that day I got flash memories of Lila's body. I remembered it as stunningly flawless, but Lila wore her beauty so casually it was disarming. What always amazed me was the symmetry of her features. I took an anatomy class in med school and of course I examine bodies and faces constantly in my work. During my six months of intimacy with Lila, I studied her beauty—as a kind of homage, I guess. I noticed little things that astonished me. Her ears, for instance, matched perfectly, her eyes, even her nostrils—almost nobody's nostrils match exactly, but hers did. Her breasts . . . I've never seen a pair sans silicone that matched like hers. And *nobody's* arms are the same size—handedness always makes one arm larger than the other—but not in Lila: she was ambidextrous. It was uncanny. If she had parted her hair in the center, you could have divided her down the middle and mirror-replicated one half and you'd have exactly the same Lila. She was that symmetrical. That's what the sixteen-year-old Naomi saw in the meadow by the stream that day, and I guess it blinded her—sort of like looking upon a goddess.

"Naomi said she had been embarrassed at first, but she followed Lila's example and stripped to her skin. They cavorted about in the pool, laughing and splashing each other but for only a short while since the water was freezing. Lila suggested they get out and lie on their clothes in the sun to warm up. Naomi felt excited and self-conscious lying next to Lila completely naked, but then, as the sun warmed her flesh, a languor spread over her, and she dozed off. When she awoke, Lila had snuggled up against her, her arm thrown over Naomi's midriff, and Lila's breast was pressed against Naomi's breast.

"Jake, this is where it got really unsettling. Naomi's voice began to change—not so hesitant any longer. More assured, more expressive, and I realized that she was taking pleasure in telling me about her seduction. As she started looking directly at me without her earlier embarrassment, I began to wonder if she knew about my affair with Lila.

"Naomi said that when she found herself in intimate physical contact with Lila, she didn't know what to do. Should she try to get up and put her clothes on? Should she roll away from Lila's embrace? She was too numb, she said, even to move her arm. So she waited to see what Lila would do. After a few minutes Lila asked, 'Are you awake, Naomi?' Naomi turned and looked into her eyes. 'You feel nice to lie against. You don't mind, do you?' Then she began to run her hand up and down Naomi's side, then across her stomach, gently massaging. After a few minutes she began to nuzzle Naomi's neck with her nose and lips. Then she kissed her—on the mouth.

"'Naomi, I feel very close to you. You are a very attractive young lady. I want to make love to you, and I think you want to make love to me. There's nothing wrong with two women enjoying each other. You'll find it's a very natural thing. Just relax. I'll guide us.'

"And she did, Jake. Lila made love to the girl—a sixteen-year-old girl. Naomi didn't tell me what they did . . . and I didn't ask. She just said that Lila had 'made love' to her. And continued to make love to her once or twice a week—sometimes in the woods, sometimes in the house—until October, around the time Naomi first saw Goon. He was staying at the ranch, and he started riding with Lila. Lila told Naomi to saddle and bridle Major every afternoon. Whenever they were together alone, Lila seemed preoccupied—she never even kissed her. They never made love again after Goon showed up. Naomi was confused and hurt, but she didn't know what to do about it. Although she kept feeding the horses and caring for the tack, she didn't see much of Lila. Then she heard that you had found Lila's body over in Golden Meadows. At first she wouldn't believe that Lila was dead. When the realization finally struck her, she couldn't grieve openly. She told me that at night she had cried silently in her bed. On other occasions she went off by herself to the barn when she knew no one else would be there and wept.

"After telling me all of this, Naomi said, 'I'm afraid, Miss Jefferson. I liked making love to Lila. Sometimes that was all I could think about. I didn't do well in school during the fall. I'm afraid that I'm a lesbian.'

"At first Naomi had felt so embarrassed when Lila touched her that she couldn't bring herself to return any of Lila's caresses. 'I just let her do it to me. Then as I got used to the excitement, I began to want to do things to her . . . and I did. I'm really worried that I'm queer. . . . Miss Jefferson, does making love with Lila make me queer?'

"Then she asked if I'd ever made love to a woman. What was I going to say? I was relieved to know that Lila had never told her about us, but I had to do something to ease the girl's mind. So I made up a story about a woman in Seattle who seduced me in much the same way Lila had seduced her. I told her I was obsessed with the woman but when we broke up after six months, I found that my attraction to men hadn't diminished, and that I hadn't had an affair with a woman since. . . . I was surprised at how easily that lie jumped off my tongue. I told her she shouldn't worry about her sexual orientation. Psychologists have shown we are all bisexual, and sometimes our attraction for someone of the same sex needs to be realized physically. I know this sounds corny, Jake, but I had to tell her something. I said that as long as love and caring for the other person were the compelling forces, then we shouldn't let episodes like that trouble us. I also told her she would go on to live a normal life—get married, have kids, and enjoy her family. . . ."

Gwen falls silent for a moment, then she says quietly, "Well, I hope she will. I hope to God she will. I hope Lila didn't screw her up for life. You can't tell with a kid that young. It was all right for Lila to put the make on me. I was thirty-one years old. Old enough to take care of myself, even if I didn't. But sixteen—that was evil. I hope that what Turrentine suggested to you about Lila's father was the truth. At least that would mitigate her lechery. But I don't know. Evil is evil—unredeemable. Maybe it's a good thing Goon killed her. She might have corrupted the whole county if she had gone on living. . . . Oh, Jake, I'm so numb I don't think I can feel anymore. I can't cry. Is this something Lila has brought on us all? Or is it just something in ourselves that Lila brought out? I'm so damned exhausted I can't think straight anymore."

I don't answer her. I don't need to answer her. She's said it all. Now she closes her eyes. I sit and watch her in the dim light. Soon her breathing begins to slow down, and the easy rhythms of sleep soften her troubled face.

Sometime in the night I awake to a dream. It is Laura come again to coax me to the warm, quiet place where she dwells.

"Come on, Jake. I'm waiting for you. You've caused enough trouble down here. You've fucked up enough lives. That student in Chicago. This new girlfriend. . . . What's her name? Gwen? You almost got her killed the other day. And that dog—he's as good as dead now. You'd better come with me where you can't do any more harm."

I get out of bed and go in the kitchen. I take out the rum and start to make a milk toddy. But I stop before I drink it. I don't need this stuff, I say to myself, and pour the contents of the glass down the sink.

Chapter Nineteen

THIS MORNING WE GET UP AT FOUR-THIRTY AND DRIVE TO GREAT FALLS to see Spook. He's lying on a gurney with full intravenous apparatus for nourishment and drugs. He's been in a coma for three days now. But his life signs haven't changed much, Dr. Johnson tells us—still fairly strong. Gwen goes over and rubs Spook's head and ears, then leans over and kisses him on the top of his head. I see her tears falling on his brow and rolling down onto his eyes.

"Don't die, Spook. You know I love you. Jake loves you. You've got to get well and come home with us."

As she raises her head, Spook opens his eyes and looks at her. His eyes are calm but beseeching, as if to say, "Yes, I want to go home too. But now I have to rest."

He looks at her for fifteen seconds or so, then closes his eyes again.

On the way back to Clark City, Gwen tries to talk calmly about Spook. "His temperature is only two degrees above normal. That means his body is dealing with the infection pretty well. I think he may pull out of it."

She continues to talk calmly, but twenty miles out of Great Falls, she breaks down and starts crying again. She sobs off and on all the way back to Clark City.

"Godammit, Jake. I know he's going to die."

When we get home, Gwen brews coffee and drinks two cups,

talking to me about the clinic, and then about how we might fix the house up this summer. Then about my cabin over in Finnegan's Gulch. Then she takes a shower.

After I walk Gwen to work, I drop by the Bunkhouse to see how Carlton is doing. He's lying on his bunk, reading the same Tony Hillerman novel.

"This guy, Jim Chee, is a pretty smart Indian, Jake. I bet he could figure out how to catch that Dimitri fellow. You and me, we just don't have enough experience in the crime business."

When he asks if Gwen is doing all right, I tell him she's fine—except for worrying herself sick about Spook—and putting all her nervous energy into her work. Then I tell him I've got a feeling something is going to break today. Goon is going to show up here in town or out at the Circle 9.

"If you'll stick around the Bunkhouse, or the Antler, I can get you pronto if things start popping. Can you do that?"

"Sure, Jake. I can't work today anyway. The snow is still two feet deep out at the Bar Ten. Can't work on that barn of Johnson's until we get some warm weather or a chinook."

I go home and fiddle around the house, wash the breakfast dishes, make the bed. I get on the computer and try to write, but the words aren't coming. My mind keeps drifting off to Spook lying there in the animal clinic. Then to Lila and Goon. My nerves are standing on edge with the feeling that something is going to break. In Vietnam I was like this every time I felt a new deployment developing somewhere in the brass's brains. I eat a small lunch, then go back to the computer. When at 1:15 the phone rings, the hair on the back of my neck stands up. I hesitate a moment, then pick up the receiver. Jeremy's voice on the other end of the line is quaking and cracking.

"Mr. Battle, you've got to get out here quick," he says, whispering fast. "He's here. He just killed Mr. Modell and Mr. Dawkins. I'm calling from Miss Lila's bedroom. I was getting ready to serve lunch when Mr. Dimitri appeared in the sunroom—like he stepped out from behind the curtains, or out of a closet. He walked right up to Modell with a pistol and shot him in the forehead. Mr. Dawkins was trying to get at his gun, but Bet shot him too. I ducked back into the kitchen and told Olivia to make herself scarce, then I climbed upstairs to call you. Mr. Turrentine was in the dining room, eating lunch with Miss Stoop. I haven't heard any more shots, and I don't know where Mr. Buck is, probably still outside patrolling. I don't know what to do. I don't have a gun up here. . . ."

The phone goes dead. Not like it does when somebody hangs up but like the whole system has failed. I call Helena and tell Barney to radio Ralston and the state police. Then I call the Bunkhouse but nobody answers the phone. I grab the .38. My .30–06 and 12-gauge are in the 4Runner. I pull on my down coat and put on heavy boots. In ten minutes I'm at the Bunkhouse. There's nobody in the lobby. I yell upstairs for Carlton, but there's no answer. I run over to the Antler. He's not there but was earlier, helping Phil and Nerice decorate for New Year's Eve. Nerice thinks Carlton and Phil are eating lunch at Janie's. I tell her what's going on and ask her to call Gwen and see if she can find Tim Free. We might need all the help we can get. Janie says Carlton and Phil left twenty minutes ago to pick up fireworks at Tommy Norwood's house. I can't wait any longer. I tell her to find Carlton and have him get out to the Circle 9 as soon as possible. Then I jump back in the 4Runner and mash the accelerator to the floor.

I can see smoke two miles before I get to the ranch, but I don't know what's burning until I clear the aspen grove two hundred yards up the lane. The upper floor of the main house is ablaze. Goon is just coming out of the garage with a gasoline can. He sloshes the contents against the front of the house, throws the can on the front stoop, then ducks around behind the garage. I turn the car broadside and stop fifty yards from the house, grab the .30-06, and slip out the door. Using the rear wheels as a shield, I peek through the canopy windows but don't see Goon anywhere. I sprint up to the house, keeping my eyes on the corners for any sign that he's watching. The house is engulfed in flames now; the garage is an inferno. Through the open door, I glimpse the Jag burning fiercely.

I look into the house through the front windows but see only smoke and flames. I flank the garage with my gun at ready. I drop down on my left knee and wait for Goon to step out from behind the house. But there's only roiling smoke and flames. I run to the corner where the kitchen and screened porch jut into the backyard and try again to look inside: nothing but fire. The heat is intense even thirty feet away from the walls. I move farther out to get clear of the billowing smoke, expecting at any moment to see Goon emerge with his gun yammering. Then I spot him—three hundred yards from the house, running toward the airstrip and Turrentine's Learjet. He probably knows how to fly it.

By the time I get to the edge of the strip, Goon has the engines started. I can see heat radiating from the nacelles and nozzles. Fortunately the plane is facing my way. As it moves toward me, I kneel and squeeze off a round at the cockpit. The plane keeps coming. I squeeze off another round. It begins to swing around in a practiced way and I realize that Goon is turning back into the wind for take-off. It also dawns on me that Turrentine probably had armored glass and shielding installed around the cockpit. I drop into prone firing position. Through my scope I have no trouble getting the engine exhaust in the crosshairs. The plane is probably two hundred fifty yards down the runway when I fire the first shot. Nothing happens. I squeeze off another. And another. The plane lurches to the right, and the engine begins to disintegrate. I can see compressor blades ripping up the cowl and fuselage. There is an explosion, causing the right wing to sag, and the longhorn wingtip drags along the concrete, spinning the plane clockwise. The engine bursts into flames.

I slip five more cartridges into the rifle and run toward the burning plane. There is no sign of Goon, but I'm ready to drop down and fire if he shows himself. I veer to the left so he can't see me from the cockpit. I'm in line with the plane's longitudinal axis when I spot him. He must have slipped out of the port hatch after the plane spun around. He's halfway to the forest high stepping through the snow about three hundred yards ahead of me. I drop on my left knee and try to line him up in the scope. But he's lurching, and I'm so winded I can't hold him in the crosshairs. I squeeze off a shot anyway. He stops and spins around. I see he has a rifle. He fires. Slugs are buzzing and screaming all across the concrete. It's an AK-47—I'd recognize that muzzle stutter anywhere. I flatten myself against the runway and cover my head with my arms, trying to make myself as thin a target as possible. There's another burst from his gun and a piece of something—probably a shard from a disintegrating bullet—whacks my shoulder but doesn't penetrate the coat. Goon fires another burst. Something hot rips through the right sleeve of my coat. My arm starts burning just above the elbow. I raise the arm several times to make sure it's still functioning. When I look back toward Goon, he's off and running again. I try to aim but it's useless. I fire twice out of frustration, then watch him disappear into a dark hole in the forest.

I lie there, exhausted. I'm getting too old for this. Thirty years have passed since my last firefight. My legs, lungs, heart are shaking, wheezing, pounding. I lie there on the concrete and watch the plane burn. Twelve million dollars of aviation high technology being reduced to scrap! Five minutes pass. I hear Carlton yelling—"Jake, Jake, you okay?" He's running toward me. When I sit up, I see several other people scurrying around up near the house.

"Just a scratch on my arm, but that son of a bitch got away into the woods. We're going to have to hunt him down," I say, still breathing hard. "He's got an AK-47 and who knows what else in his arsenal."

Carlton gives me a hand.

"Where were you? If you'd stayed at the Bunkhouse like I asked, we could have gotten the son of a bitch. . . . Oh, fuck it."

A few people are standing in the parking lot, watching the place burn.

Phil Turner comes running over. "You okay, Jake? Couldn't be anybody alive in the house. The whole place is an inferno. We checked the guesthouse and the barn. Nobody there. The telephone in the guesthouse works. I called the volunteer fire department."

As I look at the blazing house, I wonder how Jeremy and Olivia died . . . if Goon shot them or left them to burn alive. I should have made them leave the place after Goon took those shots at Gwen. I don't give a shit for most of the others. Modell and Dawkins had probably caused enough suffering to deserve what they got—a bullet in the head. Buck Wallace wasn't a bad guy: I'd even come to like him a little after listening to his story. He was just in the wrong business with the wrong people. I didn't know Iris Stoop, had never even seen her, but she must have been privy to a lot of evil if she was Turrentine's private secretary. And Turrentine … after reading Abe Isaacs' report, I'd come to think of the man as a kind of arch-villain—an attractive arch-villain but an arch-villain, nevertheless.

I look at my right sleeve; a big stain is spreading near the elbow. I pull off the coat and roll up my shirtsleeve, revealing an ugly flesh wound just below the scar I picked up in Nam. There doesn't appear to be any serious damage, and the bleeding has almost stopped. I ask Phil to wrap my bandana over the wound and secure it.

Mainly, I'm angry and frustrated.

"Get your rifle, Carlton. Bring the .38 too. Let's go get that motherfucka. Are you ready?"

"You betchum, Red Rider."

Where Goon's tracks leave the airstrip, we strap on snowshoes.

"Carlton, you've never hunted a human animal. I have, so you listen to me. This guy is dangerous. An AK-47 is a dangerous weapon. You've got to respect its firepower. Goon may even have another Bizon 2 with him. And probably a sidearm. I want you to stay about thirty yards to my left and behind me. Watch me for signals. If I give the signal to hit the ground, find a big tree and get behind it. And remember, we are tracking an intelligent animal. He could set an ambush. He may circle back and be waiting for us. He could even be up in a tree, so look everywhere."

As we begin to track, I realize it won't take long to catch up with Goon. The snow hasn't melted as much in the woods as out in the open. Where the terrain dips, it's often four feet deep. On the level, it's a good foot and a half. Even with his long legs, Goon is going to have a hard time without snowshoes post-holing through the drifts. I move deliberately, not too fast, using my eyes like searchlights. I scan from right to left, against the normal visual flow, to make any disturbance or unnatural object jump out from the landscape. It's a trick I discovered in Vietnam, and it served me well in jungle combat. But Goon doesn't have any telltale color on: no red or blue or orange. He has gray pants and a khaki jacket, though I think my eyes can pick up the khaki.

Half an hour later, his tracks still aim due west through the woods. I guess we're getting closer, but there's no way to tell. Ahead is a ridge, the first of any size we've seen. Much of the snow has blown off the crest, making it a natural pathway. My guess is that he's turned south and is following the ridge since it angles away from us in that direction, but from here I can't tell. I signal Carlton that I'm going to bear left at an angle that will save us distance and time if I'm right.

Sure enough, when we get to the ridge, Goon's tracks follow the crest. I can see them fifty yards ahead. I can also see a knoll with a rock outcropping two or three hundred yards beyond. If I were Goon, that's where I'd set my ambush He must realize that he can't keep pace in this snow much longer. I signal for Carlton to move out to the left. He sees the rock outcropping and nods. Lodgepole pine and spruce are spaced along the ridge, forming an open park. I angle twenty yards to the right and begin to move forward, from the cover of one tree to the next. I'm within thirty yards of the rocks when I catch sight of a little patch of khaki between two large boulders. I signal Carlton to stop and take cover, but when I see the rifle barrel, I think it's too late. I leap to the right behind a big pine just as a burst from the AK-47 tears bark off a tree behind me. I hear a shot from Carlton's .270. When I peek out from behind the tree, the rifle barrel and the khaki patch are gone. I scan the rocks. Nothing moving. I move forward slowly. Just as I get to the knoll the AK-47 speaks again, but not in my direction. There's a long silence, then Carlton calls out that he's been hit.

"Christ, he got me in the leg. . . . I don't think it's too bad."

I can see Goon trying to cross a draw to the west but can't get a bead on him.

Another burst splatters off the rocks above where Carlton is lying.

"You okay, Carlton?"

"I'm okay. He can't see me from where he is."

I move quickly up onto the knoll using the rocks for cover. When I look out to the west, Goon is climbing up the other side of the draw. Just as I get a bead on him, a big spruce gets in the way. I can see only his left leg. I aim at the back of the knee. When the slug hits him, he lets out a bloodcurdling bellow, savage and forlorn, like some mammoth the Paleo-Indians have surrounded and wounded.

On the second day of assault on Hill 937, my platoon is assigned to clear out a line of approach to the NVA fortifications. We are looking for snipers and forward observers. Lambert is a new replacement. I tell him to stay behind and to my right as we move up a shallow wash. We've just come out of the wash onto a bench when a sniper takes out two of our men about forty meters to the right. Lambert spots the sniper in a big palm and empties his whole clip into the fronds. The gook topples out of the tree like a sack, hits the ground and bounces. Lambert is excited. It's his first kill. He runs toward the body. I try to yell him back, but it's too late. He's leaning proudly over the gook when the grenade goes off. I had never seen a body fold backward on itself before. It looked as if Lambert had been split down the middle and his two sides, his arms and shoulders, had closed backward like a busted paperback.

From where I'm crouched behind a rock, I can't see Carlton and I don't want to call to him. I hope he knows what to do about his leg. After five minutes I still see no sign of Goon. I saw him go down, but he must be hiding behind the spruce waiting for me to show myself. Just as I move to the right, another burst from the AK-47 splatters off the rock in front of me. One slug whines by so close to my ear I think for a moment I must have been hit. But when I touch the side of my head, there's no blood. I catch a glimpse of Goon's khaki jacket to the right of the tree and dive behind a rock just as another burst rattles all around me. When I look again, Goon has disappeared. Shit. Why didn't I see him before I moved? Thirty years—I've lost the edge Charlie ground onto my instincts. I slide down behind a boulder, then back off the knoll, using it as a shield to move far to my right. When I come out of the ravine I might have an angle to see him. He probably expects I'll stay in the safety of the boulders.

I move up, careful to stay hunched over, then take off my snowshoes and wallow to the top of the ridge. Sure enough I can see a patch of khaki, but it disappears and I can see only his boot and lower leg. I could shoot his foot, but that won't accomplish anything. He's already disabled. I'd just give away my new position. I wait. Five. . . ten minutes. Slowly he moves his head from behind the tree. I can tell he's scanning the snow up toward the knoll, looking for tracks or other clues to where I am. I almost get a bead on him before he pulls his head back behind the tree. It must be down around zero, and he's wearing only that thin khaki jacket. How the hell does he keep from freezing? He's probably lost some blood too. Probably getting pretty numb. Another ten minutes. He pokes his head out from behind the tree again, like an old terrapin. I get his temple in the crosshairs this time and twist the scope up to ten power. In the few seconds it takes me to steady on his head I register his face: He *is* an ugly bastard. None of his features seem to match. One small ear lies close in against his head, the other, much larger, juts out like an open car door. His left eye is noticeably higher than the right. His right cheekbone sags. His nose is flattened to the right.

He must feel the gun on him and begins to scan toward me. I think he sees me just as I squeeze off the round.

He looks dead, so I move in. Twenty yards away, I see his brains blown all over the snow. I kick his AK-47 away and frisk him. He has a P-38 pistol and five full thirty-round AK-47 clips in his pockets. He's cut the left sleeve off his shirt and made a tourniquet just above the left knee, which is torn all to hell. If he'd lived, the lower leg would have had to come off. Carnage. Blood and brains as bad as I'd witnessed in the war. I expect the old reaction to set in. Nausea. Disgust and trembling. But it doesn't come. I'm still strung tight as a bottom E-string, but there's no stomach-wrenching revulsion.

I call to Carlton to tell him Goon is dead. Then I go over to see how he's doing. The bullet went through his right thigh, probably hitting the femur, but it doesn't feel broken. He doesn't feel much pain and isn't bleeding badly. I tear the tail off my shirt and bandage the leg loosely.

"You sure he's dead, Jake? He's not going to get up and start shooting again?"

"He's dead. His brains are spread over fifty square feet."

I tell Carlton to hold on while I go back to pack the body in snow. Ralston can bring in a crew later to carry him out. I dig a hole in the snow two feet deep with my hands and rifle stock and roll Goon into it. He is heavy—real dead weight. He comes to rest face up. The 180-grain lead slug made only a small hole in his forehead, right in the middle like a Hindu caste mark, but it didn't leave much of the back of his head when it came out. His eyes are open, staring off into space. In death he is more hideous than any monster Hollywood could ever devise. No wonder he scared the hell out of so many people. I leave his eyes open and pile snow on top of his body. Maybe the carcajou won't find him before Ralston comes to retrieve the corpse. I take the AK-47, remove the clip, jack the cartridge out of the chamber, and jam the barrel into the snow to mark where he's buried. Then I go back to get Carlton.

We leave our rifles propped against a tree. With his right arm over my shoulder and a pine sapling to brace with, we make fair progress back over our trail. About halfway to the airstrip, we meet Ralston, Tim Free, and a posse of ten men.

"So you got him," Ralston says. "I was hoping I'd be the one who took him out. But it's only fitting you got the privilege."

"Some privilege, Ralston. I hope I never get such a privilege again. I hope I remain underprivileged for the rest of my life."

Tim Free comes over to help me with Carlton.

"Easy," I say. "He's got a nasty little .308 hole in his leg."

I recount for Ralston how we had tracked Goon and cornered him on a knoll. How he had almost caught me with his first burst. How he had wounded Carlton after Carlton shot at him.

"I guess I shouldn't have taken that shot, Jake. But I was trying to distract him from you. I saw the bark flying off that tree. I guess I gave myself away."

"You did distract him. If I hadn't seen his rifle muzzle just before he fired, I'd be the corpse now instead of Goon. His second burst might have hit me. Your shot got him looking away from my position."

I tell Ralston where to look for Goon's body and ask him to bring our rifles when they come out. Then Tim and I get our arms around Carlton on either side and walk him back to the airstrip. Gus Fox and Gwen are waiting there with the ambulance. We can see that there isn't much left of the house, even though the fire department is still pumping water onto the smoking ruins. The Learjet looks like a giant gutted grasshopper.

"You okay, Jake? When I heard you and Carlton had gone after Dimitri, I had a premonition of the rescue squad bringing both of you out in body bags. You seem all right?"

I assure her that I'm fine and ask her to take a look at Carlton's leg. She tells us what I had suspected—that the bullet probably took a sliver out of the femur.

"We need to get him to Great Falls for an x-ray."

She cleans and dresses the wound and gives him a shot of antibiotic. Since Carlton's not badly hurt and is obviously not suffering from shock, Gwen asks Gus to drive him to the hospital without her.

"I don't think there will be any others to take," she says. "Looks like whoever was in the house won't even require cremation. But you can never tell."

Gwen and I ride with Gus over to the guesthouse, which the rescue squad has set up as an aid and recovery station. She has a look at my wound—nothing serious—outlines it with antiseptic, and dresses it. After warming up, we walk over to the main house. It is nearly six o'clock, and night has settled around us. Spotlights from the rescue squad and fire department are focused all over the walls. Warning lights from the fire engine, police cars, and rescue vehicles cast blinking, swirling blue and lurid-red dyes across the parking area. The roof of the house is almost entirely gone, but the outer and inner walls are still standing. A team of five professional firefighters has come out from Helena with Ralston's entourage. They say there is no chance of survivors in the rubble and not much they can do until morning. It would be too dangerous to go into the house: The floors might give way, or the walls might collapse. Tomorrow they can bring an engineer out from Helena to assess the structural damage before going in to retrieve what is left of the bodies.

Newspaper reporters and TV crews begin to arrive. They ask a lot of questions, but I tell them they'll have to wait for Ralston to bring in Goon's body before we tell the story. By seven, there are a hundred people milling around the parking area, but the temperature is dropping rapidly—the rescue chief tells me it's fifteen below zero—so most of the media personnel go into the guesthouse to warm and revive themselves with coffee. At eight-thirty, Ralston and the posse arrive with Goon's body. They have had to double up his legs to make him fit in a body bag. He's loaded in the rescue squad's ambulance and sent off to the morgue in Helena. By 10 p.m. Ralston has given the press the official story and I've made myself scarce so I won't have to appear on camera.

Since there's nothing left to do, most everybody leaves to find shelter and food. The Bunkhouse and Covered Wagon Motel will be full-up tonight. A few of the volunteer fireman are still pumping water on the smoking ruins; they've run a flexible pipe a hundred yards down to the retaining pond in a shallow draw at the north end of the grounds and have knocked a big hole in the ice. Ralston comes over to say he's heading back to Helena: "I'm taking my people with me. Nobody can do any good out here tonight."

We agree that since I'll be the only law left in Clark City, I'll stay in the guesthouse to make sure no souvenir hunters get into the ruins. Gwen wants to stay with me.

"We'll hold down the fort until you get back with your crew tomorrow morning."

"I'll close the gate at the road," he says, "and put some 'keep out—crime scene' tape across it. Maybe that will help."

He tells the volunteer firemen they can go home. They leave the fire truck, pipes, and hoses in place and pile into Bill Tomaski's Montero and head back to town.

After everyone leaves, Gwen and I walk over to the ruins. A few flames are still flickering here and there, but we can't see much, so we go back to the guesthouse. The rescue squad has left us some sandwiches and coffee, but neither of us is hungry.

"I'm still keyed up, Jake. I know you are too. But we need the sleep. Tomorrow is going to be another troubling day."

We go into the master bedroom. Olivia's meticulous housekeeping has not been disturbed. Fresh, ironed sheets are on the bed. The carpet is fluffed and pristine. Fresh towels are stacked neatly in the bathroom. Since the other two bedrooms are upstairs, I'm sure this is where Buck Wallace spied on Lila and Goon. I try to picture their coupling, but the images my mind produces are too hideous to bear: Lila's face is mangled, and maggots are seething in her wounds; the back of Goon's monstrous head is blown away. I don't know how long I lie awake with images upon images whirling around in my head: Lila and Gwen, Lila and Naomi, Lila and Goon, Lila dead and rotting in a shallow grave, Goon with half his head blown out, and then Randal and Iris Stoop, Buck and Modell and Scott Dawkins burned to little piles of ash. And worse, Jeremy and Olivia. . . . I feel a chill numbing my bones and gut. I start trembling, but I can't weep. I pull Gwen against me and bury my face in her neck until I finally drift off to sleep.

Sometime during the night a crashing sound wakes us.

"What the hell was that, Jake?"

We go to the window and look at what's left of the big house. There's a tiny sliver of moon and the luminescence of snow to furnish a little light. The wall of the house facing us has collapsed. There's nothing we can do about that, so we go back to bed.

Later I awake to the feeling of Gwen's arm pulling on my shoulder.

"Did another wall fall?" I say.

"No, there's somebody in trouble . . . out there at the house. I can hear voices."

I lie there for a few seconds, straining to hear. But the only sound is from the refrigerator in the next room. How can there be anybody alive out there, much less in trouble? Perhaps some thrill seeker or souvenir hunter has gotten into the ruins and hurt himself. I look at the clock. It's five minutes to eight.

"Come on, get dressed. We'll go see."

Wide awake now, I pull on my clothes. Out the window the world is beginning to brighten. By the time we get outdoors, it's almost sunrise. As we walk toward the ruins, a breeze stiffens in our faces and an inner wall of the house topples, spewing a cloud of dirt and ash in our direction. As the dust settles the sun begins to peek above the world's rim, and a fantastic tableau emerges. At first we can't imagine what we're seeing. We remember the floor plan well enough to know we're looking into the kitchen, a single-story addition at the back of the structure. The roof is incompletely burned, but the back wall, which had been floor-to-ceiling windows, is completely blown away. As the sun illuminates the interior, we see a central figure sitting in a chair. Around it are blobs curled on the floor. From the right a crystal-like plume arcs four or five feet out from the wall and attaches itself to the chair.

I can't decipher the scene for some moments. Then I realize that the figure is a body coated in ice. The kitchen sink has fallen to the floor, leaving the severed pipes exposed and creating a fountain that must have cascaded over the body, turning it into a gruesome icy sculpture when the house was no longer hot enough to keep the water from freezing. Ice also covers the kitchen floor, which rests on a thick concrete slab. How deep we cannot tell, but the ice holds the several heaps in its grasp. As we move forward, sunlight seems to explode from the encrusted figure on the chair. Unmistakably, it is Turrentine. I can make out his profile and his charred body without hair or clothes—a naked embryo encased in a crystalline sac. The exterior of the casing is as smooth and unblemished as a glass sculpture. The water must have frozen and melted over and over as the flames diminished. Now the ice acts as a gigantic lens, refracting the sun in spectacular shafts of light.

The extravagant display lasts for only a minute, but the icy fetus continues to glitter as the sun rises higher. By its radiance I see four blobs arranged in an irregular semicircle in front of Turrentine's chair.

"Over here," Gwen says. "That's where the voices are coming from."

She leads the way around the house. I follow, although I hear nothing.

She stops at the rear of the kitchen, beside what's left of the screened porch.

"I think they're down here."

"Where?"

"Somewhere under the concrete."

"How could they be down there?"

"I don't know. But that's where they are."

Then I hear a voice from somewhere farther in the house: "Is anyone there?"

I am astounded.

"Is that you, Jeremy?"

"Yes, Mr. Battle. It's me. Olivia is down here too. In the old bomb shelter. But there aren't any stairs left up from the cellar. Maybe you could get that ladder we keep down in the barn."

It takes half an hour, but finally I get the ladder across the ice on the kitchen floor and angle it down into the gaping hole that is the uncovered basement. We coax Olivia up first. I help her across the icy floor to Gwen, who hurries her over to the guesthouse to examine her and make sure she's okay. Because of his bulk, Jeremy has a difficult time climbing out. I have to brace myself against a charred timber and give him a hand so he can slip around the extended horns of the ladder. As we cross the kitchen floor, he takes it all in.

"Lord-a-mercy, Mr. Battle. All them dead. Mr. Turrentine. I don't think I'll ever get over it. Mr. Turrentine, he was always good to me. Always good to me. Lord-a-mercy. Lord-a- mercy."

He starts to weep, silently, big tears rolling down his cheeks.

When we get to the guesthouse, Gwen has Olivia lying on the bed wrapped in blankets, and says that she seems okay. No burns. Just exhaustion and mild shock.

"Now you come here, Jeremy. Take off your shirt so I can examine you."

She pushes a stethoscope into the layers of fat on his chest and then his back, and listens intently.

"My god, Jeremy. Your heart is healthy as a horse's. How do you keep it that way with all your fat? We're going to have to do something about that fat. . . . Now put your shirt back on and lie down there beside Olivia. I'll cover you with a blanket. I don't think you're in shock. But I want you to rest."

"I'm fine, Miss Jefferson. I'm fine. But I will lie down for a minute. That climb out of the cellar sort of got me bushed."

Gwen and I leave them and shut the door. Ten minutes later, Ralston, Barney, Tim Free, the coroner, and two state policemen arrive, followed a few minutes later by five Helena firemen and the volunteer squad from Clark City.

"My God, Jake!" Ralston exclaims. "You mean to tell me somebody survived that fire!"

I explain about the old bomb shelter beneath the concrete slab of the porch. "Jeremy said it was made to survive a holocaust. I guess the fire wasn't much test of its capabilities."

"That's a miracle, Jake. And guess what. Another miracle. All our computers were working this morning. The TV says everybody pulled through all right. I guess that Y2K scare was just that—a scare."

Carlton is okay too, Ralston reports. The doctors had to do a little cutting, so he'll be in the hospital for a couple of days. "But he says to tell you he's fine."

The media folks begin to arrive, about twenty of them altogether, some from national TV. Turrentine's death is big news. They set up cameras and photograph the crew removing the bodies. Gwen and I don't go out to watch, but Ralston tells me they have to use a pickax to chop the corpses out of the ice. They chip Turrentine out with survival knives. I guess they won't thaw the bodies until they're at the morgue in Helena.

Everybody wants interviews—with me and Ralston. When they find out about the survival of Olivia and Jeremy, they want immediately to interview them. Gwen says that will have to wait until they're rested; she has to make sure they've recovered from their ordeal.

When Gwen brings them out at eleven, Olivia won't talk to any of the reporters, but Jeremy agrees to tell his story. He sits in a chair with all the cameras on him and news-people gathered around.

"Yes, sir, I saw that Dimitri shoot Mr. Modell and Mr. Dawkins. I don't know where he came from. He just appeared. Walked right up to Mr. Modell and shot him in the head. Shot Mr. Dawkins when he went for his gun. He had one of those silencers on his pistol. That's when I climbed upstairs and called Mr. Battle. I didn't get much time. Mr. Dimitri came up after me and tore the phone cord out of the wall. He took me downstairs to the dining room, where I saw he had stripped Mr. Turrentine and tied him to a chair. He had already shot Miss Stoop. A few minutes later he dragged in Mr. Buck. He had killed him earlier somewhere outside. Then he took me and Olivia and locked us in the closet back in the hall. We were in there for half an hour or so when I smelled the smoke and I knew that Mr. Dimitri had set the place on fire and Olivia and I were going to burn to a crisp unless I got us out of there.

"I made Olivia sit in the back corner of the big closet—it's sort of a pantry—and braced myself against the back shelves and started kicking at the door panel next to the hinges. It took a bunch of kicks, but I finally broke through. Then I went to work on the hinge pins with a screwdriver I found in the closet. When I finally got them out, the house was burning hot—flames were everywhere we looked. I grabbed Olivia—she was nearly passed out from the heat and smoke—and took her down the stairs to the basement. I had discovered the bomb shelter shortly after Mr. Turrentine brought me to Montana, and figured it was built back when someone added the screened-in porch. I dragged Olivia into the shelter and shut both of the insulated steel doors—one of them is like those sealed doors you see on ships. Once we were safely inside, I wasn't too worried about the fire, knowing there was an air shaft that came up next to the big birdbath in the backyard. The shelter was equipped with everything we needed to survive for a couple of months: big glass bottles of distilled water, canned food, blankets. Let me tell you, I gave plenty of thanks to the Lord while we were down there. He provided for Olivia and me—air, water, everything you could think to want—but I guess he had different plans for Mr. Turrentine and his people. I prayed for their souls, for I knew they had departed this Earth. Maybe it was the Lord's wrath that was visited upon them. I don't know. I loved Mr. Turrentine, but he was surely mixed up in some evil doings. . . . Mr. Battle here, he's my friend. I guess he delivered us all from that devil Dimitri. The Lord be praised for our deliverance."

Epilogue

YES: THE LORD—WHOEVER OR WHATEVER HE IS—BE PRAISED. HIS—at least the Christian *his*—third millennium has arrived, without much fuss despite the dire predictions. Today marks summer solstice of the year two thousand. The world is green, particularly green this year. In May and early June, the rains fell, then the warm sun stirred the earth: As Rilke says, prodigal spring came in like a child who has learned her poems by heart. The cottonwood and aspen are aflutter with new life. Wildflowers have inundated our prairies. We are gathered—all my friends and neighbors—at my cabin on the edge of the wilderness. Carlton and I have raised the logs and put on the roof, the fireplace and chimney are half laid up, but the cabin isn't yet habitable. We've borrowed three outfitters' tents and a big dining canopy from Johnson Clyde. He's also donated a cow—a bison cow—which he and Gus Fox have been cooking over a freshly dug barbecue pit since noon yesterday.

Jeremy and Olivia were here for a couple of hours earlier today. They brought a ten-gallon pot of tamales Olivia made for the occasion. They wanted to stay but had to get back to their restaurant in Helena. Yes, their restaurant—Gwen and I helped with the financing. They've been open for three months. It's taken a while, but the folks in Helena have finally "discovered" *La Tertulia*. It's sure a hundred cuts above the Tex-Mex chains out on the strip. Already they're showing a profit. Jeremy has also installed a piano and plays every night from five to seven. He admitted to me in January that he'd been practicing on the baby grand at the Circle 9 for several years. Although he hasn't recovered his early facility—his fingers are still too stiff—he can do the basic stuff. The rhythm is still there, and his instinct for chordal structure. He and Olivia were married in May. I was best man and Gwen was maiden of honor—well not quite "maiden." She was five months pregnant with our child. She's beginning to swell nicely. Very healthy. Very handsome. We plan to get married in September after the baby arrives. Also, we've finally gotten Jeremy and Olivia to call me "Jake" and Gwen "Gwen," instead of "Mr. Battle" and "Miss Jefferson."

About the bomb shelter that saved Jeremy and Olivia: I wrote Larry Thompson in Tucson, asking who'd built the shelter and why. He said that in the 1950s, when the government was installing missile silos along the Rocky Mountain Front with their attendant command centers, Larry's father had become apprehensive, believing the area would be a prime target for Russian missiles and bombers. He built the bomb shelter according to specifications provided by the Department of Defense. When Larry was a kid, his father had subjected the family to "drills." Once they stayed in the shelter for three days to test all the features. Larry was happy to hear it had finally served its function and saved lives, though fortunately not from the threat against which it was originally constructed.

Dimitri Ivanovich Sulamanov was never officially identified. No agency in the Americas or Europe could match his fingerprints or any record with that name. There were plenty of identifying marks on his body. The coroner found ten bullet scars. Six of the slugs were still in his flesh—two from Lila's .32 and one from Gwen's .25. Part of his lower jaw had been reconstructed with metal where a slug had shattered the bone and teeth. But without a reference file, those scars were as immaterial as his fingerprints. The FBI tried to identify the language Dimitri used on the voice tape I'd copied off Gwen's machine. When they failed, I sent another copy to a friend of mine in the Linguistics Department at Chicago. He consulted a number of fellow experts. Although they couldn't be absolutely certain, the consensus was the language was that of a tribe from the upper Euphrates River Valley. It was a language considered "dead," since the last known member of the tribe had died in 1910. A British philologist, however, had recorded the tongue in some detail in the 1870s. How Dimitri came by the language is as much a mystery as his reasons for wreaking vengeance on Randal Turrentine and his minions.

The lawyers for the Turrentine estate put the Circle 9 on the market this spring. Once again, Clark City was worried about new owners coming in and shutting themselves and the ranch off from the community. A real estate developer from Arizona put in a bid, intending to subdivide the property into "ranchettes." But we've subverted that threat. Since all my money had been resting heavily on my conscience for the last two years, I formed a pact with the Nature Conservancy in Helena. I put up one million seven hundred thousand dollars. The Turrentine estate has agreed to absorb one and a half million as loss—part of which was money designated as my reward for having identified and brought to justice Lila's murderer. The Conservancy is raising the rest. It will manage the property for several years, then turn it over to the Forest Service to be added to the Lewis and Clark National Forest, which it abuts. We've also worked out conservation easements with the surrounding property owners. There are plans to make it an American bison range.

Gwen has taken Carlton's kids—Brian and Eppie—up the creek fishing. They are here for the summer. I think their mother was happy to be relieved of their care; she has just acquired a third husband. All month we've been taking turns entertaining the kids when Carlton feels he has to work. Right now he is off walking in the forest with his new girlfriend, Carla. She teaches Blackfoot cultural history at the high school in Browning. She's a slim, pretty girl, twenty-five years old. Carlton wants to show her some newly sprouted plants higher up Finnegan's Gulch that his grandmother told him were used by the traditional Blackfoot people to invigorate the blood.

Nearly a hundred townsfolk are milling around, drinking beer and talking. We've iced down six big washtubs full. That's all I drink anymore: beer and a little wine. Since Gwen stopped drinking altogether in January, I've reduced my consumption to two beers a day. But on a festive occasion like this, maybe I'll have a couple of extras. I hope there's plenty for everybody—they keep arriving in droves.

Ralston Nichols has just arrived. He and Tim Free are organizing the horseshoe-throwing competition. And the swing band from Great Falls—the Charlie Russell Wranglers—is warming up. The cabin deck is the bandstand, and we marked off a large flat area in front for dancing. Under the dining canopy down near the barbecue pit, a dozen women are laying out the food everybody brought on covered tables we borrowed from the Community Church Sunday School. There's potato salad, seven-bean salad, sliced tomatoes and cucumbers, fresh roasted ears of corn, butter beans, pickled beets and snap beans, casseroles. Whole-wheat rolls and hamburger and hot dog buns for the kids. Cakes, pies, cookies. Watermelon. Lemonade and iced tea. There are even three hand-churns of ice cream being turned down by the creek. As old Homer used to say, "There are many good things to eat."

The sun has set and night is creeping over the valley—though at this latitude this time of year, twilight lingers until nearly midnight. Most of the crowd has gone back to town or returned to their ranches. The guitarist from Russell's Wranglers is still here, playing for Gus Fox and a group of would-be singers down at the barbecue pit. They are a bit beery but high-spirited. In fact, they sound pretty good: "There's a Long, Long Trail A-Winding," "Bury Me Not on the Lone Prairie," "Tumbleweed," "Shall We Gather at the River." Tim Free even attempted a rendition of "Ghost Riders in the Sky" a while ago.

Gwen and I sit on the hewn bench beside the cabin listening. Spook is curled at our feet. Oh, yes, he survived. Gus Johnson said that when he went into the clinic New Year's morning, Spook was trying to get up from the gurney where he was strapped down. By the end of the week, he was up and walking. Now he's as healthy as he's ever been. And as smart and protective. He looks up from time to time to make sure we are okay. Carlton, Carla, and the two kids are lying on a blanket in front of their tent. The stars are beginning to burn pinholes in the velvet sky. Venus is hovering over the mountains. And to the north, Polaris—the star that does not move—is gaining power. There is even a wavering of color in the north, perhaps a prelude to an auroral display later tonight.

Gwen looks up at me, inviting a kiss. We linger, lip on lip—"The lark's on the wing. . . ." Omar and Pippa should be here. Perhaps they are. At least for right now, the world seems almost perfect. We have no illusions: there will be other threats to our spiritual well-being—other Turrentines, other Lilas, other Dimitris. There will also be the recurring self-torment for our own misdeeds and failings. But "for right now," as Ruby Archeleta says to Charlie Bloom at the end of one of my favorite movies, "Isn't it great!"

THE END

Keen Butterworth

Keen Butterworth was born and raised in Tidewater Virginia, south of the James. He graduated from Randolph-Macon College, served three and a half years on board ship as a Navy officer, taught high school in Petersburg, Virginia, for three years, and then attended graduate school at the University of South Carolina. He taught in the English department at South Carolina from 1970 until 2009. He now divides his year between Columbia, South Carolina, and Santa Fe, New Mexico, where he and his wife, Nancy, bought a house in 2011.

Made in the USA
Charleston, SC
10 March 2015